To my husband, Mac.
As long as I'm with you,
I am home

'Home is where one starts from.'
T. S. Eliot

EXT. NOTTINGHAM - DAY

July: the last day of term. A quiet road on a council house estate in St Ann's, Nottingham. A BOY dressed in school uniform, with a rucksack slung over his shoulders, turns the corner, coming into view. He saunters alone down the street and stops outside the new, red-brick Expressions community centre.

He notices the shutters of the centre are down and there is nobody around. He looks at the empty plastic wallet still fixed to the fancy railings.

All the entry forms for the screenwriting competition he was thinking about entering have now gone.

> BOY
> (*mutters to himself*)
> Probably a posh kid from Mapperley Top will win it, anyway. Who cares?

He scowls and kicks the railings.

A sharp movement near the centre's large

refuse bins grabs his attention and he steps
back to the edge of the pavement, craning
his neck to see past the bins that are
clustered there.

                    BOY
                (*calls out*)
              Hey! Who's there?

Nobody answers.

                    BOY
                 (*shouts*)
     I know someone's been stealing from this
        building. I - I'll call the police.

The BOY's head whips round at the growl of
a powerful engine and a loud, thumping bass
beat.

The BOY looks up and down the road to see
where it's coming from but the road is still
free of cars.

He hears voices shouting over the music so
he stands still and listens.

VOICE ONE

Just get in and let's go. He's in the
building right now, nicking all the
equipment. We need to get the stuff loaded
in the car and go.

VOICE TWO

Is he in the centre now? Who is it, what's
his name? (*Low voices and then laughing.*)
No way! Is he the one who's smashed all the
windows, too?

VOICE ONE

I'll tell you all about it later. In the
car, let's go.

Slamming of doors shuts off the music. The
road is quiet again.

Alarmed, the BOY steps back off the pavement
and walks backwards a few steps, into the
road. He cranes his neck to try and see
round the slight bend.

A powerful engine suddenly revs, the
screeching of tyres. The BOY sees a blur of
black-and-silver metal hurtling towards him.

3

Instinctively, the BOY turns and throws himself towards the pavement, but it is too late.

The BOY cries out as his feet leave the floor and a searing pain envelops his legs and hips.

The sound of loud, thumping music fills his ears and he squeezes his eyes shut as a massive silver grille bears down on him, screeching to a halt just inches away and level with his face.

Everything goes black for a few seconds.

CUT TO:
The BOY opens his eyes. His cheek presses into the rough asphalt of the pavement. A tall shadow looms over him.

                    SHADOWY FIGURE'S VOICE
                      (*panicked whisper*)
Oh no . . . is he . . . what if he's dead?

                    VOICE TWO
                (*urgent whisper*)
        He's breathing. Look, his eyelids are
                    flickering.

The BOY hears the sound of footsteps, and
the two figures stand aside. Then a new
figure appears.

The BOY opens his eyes slightly. His sight
is blurred but he can see a new figure
towering above him and a pair of training
shoes close to his head. It's a big effort
to keep his eyes open but the BOY squints
and tries to focus on the tiny, glistening
object on the shoe nearest to him. It's
hopeless; he quickly loses focus again.
Everything blurs.

                    NEW VOICE
                (*hoarse whisper*)
                    Leave him.

                    VOICE TWO
                (*concerned*)
        But . . . we can't just leave him.
                    What if –

                    VOICE THREE
                 (*forceful whisper*)
               I said - leave him.

Feet scuffle close by. Car doors slam. An
engine roars.

The BOY is alone.

He closes his eyes and everything goes black
again.

END SCENE.

Journal Entry – July

Name: Calum Brooks
Age: 14

The school counsellor, Freya, has given me a brand-new notebook. It's one of those posh ones wrapped in cellophane.

Freya says I have to write in it every day, and that the most important thing to remember is to be completely honest, but the sort of thing I start thinking about is just stuff that nobody else would be interested in.

'Write whatever comes into your head and don't censor your feelings. If you want to write swear words or get mad and scrawl out a whole page, then that's OK,' Freya says in her soft Irish accent. 'It's your journal, Calum, so anything goes.'

Apparently, if she tells anybody else what we talk about, she'll be breaking some kind of counselling code and it could get her fired. 'I want you to know it's completely confidential,' she assures me again.

If the teachers were more laid-back like Freya, I might try a bit harder in class.

But I don't mind writing; in fact I really like it. And there's not much else to do now I'm stuck in this crummy flat with a broken leg.

Sometimes I make up scripts in my head, like I'm

writing a proper scene from a film. See, that's what I'd like to be: *a screenwriter.*

I know, I know. Despite what Sergei and Amelia say, it's a pretty stupid idea.

You don't see those sorts of vacancies down the jobcentre.

But I can't move and I'm bored out of my skull since the accident . . . so what have I got to lose?

Two Weeks Earlier

Mr Fox's room feels cold, and his booming voice echoes around the pale green, glossed walls so even though we're standing in a line, he seems to be all around us, all at once.

'You should all be ashamed of yourselves,' he says for the third time.

From where I'm standing at the end of the line, I can see the playing fields out of the small, paned window. The grass looks marshy and needs a cut. Some of the white markings on the pitch have worn away, leaving broken lines and fractured arcs that don't really mean anything any more.

Mr Fox is talking about integration and embracing change, and how this is 'the fabric our school has been built upon all these years'. Blah, blah, blah.

The wall in front of us is covered in dated black-and-white prints. Dusty frames containing old photographs of staff who must surely now be dead, and groups of smart young students who will now be old and grey.

I wonder briefly if in another fifty years, there will be boys who aren't even born yet, stood here in this very room getting a lecture like we are.

Mr Fox thumps the edge of his desk with his hand and glares at each of us in turn.

When he looks at me, I blink and scuff the toe of my shoe on the dark wiry carpet beneath my feet.

I can't say anything to Mr Fox in front of the others, but it's just not fair if *I* get excluded.

I just stood at the back of the group like I always do.

I didn't do any of the actual bullying.

We are stuck in Mr Fox's office for another twenty minutes trying to convince him of our innocence, but in the end, he issues all four of us with fixed-term exclusions.

I get kicked out for a day, Harry and Jack get two days each, and this time Linford is out for three days.

'I could have been harder on you all, but I've decided to be lenient on this occasion . . . on the proviso you sign up to see the school counsellor.' Mr Fox scowls. 'A warning. Next time you're in front of me – and there had better not be a next time – I'll be looking at permanent exclusions.'

He looks at Linford.

To be honest, I think Mr Fox is being really hard on us. I mean, the new lad was up on his feet in no time and once he stopped feeling dizzy, he just walked back to class. OK, he had a few bumps and bruises but nothing serious, not like when Linford kicked Karl Bingham so hard in the leg he fell off the climbing wall and broke his ankle.

Dad is working down south until Thursday, so when Mr Fox's exclusion letter drops through the letterbox, I'll just rip it up. Dad will be blissfully unaware that I've been in trouble at school.

I suppose that's *one* advantage to him working away most of the week.

In all the good films, people live in exciting places – the posh areas of London or America. Places I've never been and probably never will go because we live *here*.

Our flat in Nottingham is in St Ann's; an area that's been classed as 'deprived' by the government. What they really mean is that it's a dump, a slum-hole and best avoided by your average, decent person. People sort of get stuck here and your dreams get stuck too. *Dreams of the Deprived*: sounds like a pretty miserable movie title, doesn't it?

The people who actually live here don't call it deprived. We call it home.

It might not look it, with its boarded-up pubs and dated housing, but St Ann's is an OK place to be and most of our neighbours are decent. Folks might not drive fancy cars and wear top designer gear round here, but they're 'salt of the earth', as Grandad used to say.

We've got our problems like everywhere else, but

11

those of us who've lived around here for a long time, well I suppose we sort of look out for each other.

Like last year, when Dad was working down south for ten days.

★

EXT. ST ANN'S - DAY
Council Estate, December. Freezing cold,
snowing, no cars on road. Everything covered
in a blanket of fresh snow. Silent.

Starving BOY walks down road in knee-deep
snow and hammers on door of first-floor
flat.

MRS BREWSTER
(*from inside flat*)
Who the flippin' hell is it?

BOY
It's me, Calum, from number five.

MRS BREWSTER opens door. Hair in rollers,
floral headscarf, ash on her cigarette a
centimetre long. Pokes head out and squints
at the bright whiteness.

12

MRS BREWSTER

What ya standing there wi' ya gob wide open
for?

BOY

Errm . . . the Happy Shopper has run out of
milk and bread.

(Starving BOY neglects to mention Dad is
away and money has run out.)

MRS BREWSTER
(*with a sympathetic smile*)
Just a sec.

Moments later, she reappears at door.

MRS BREWSTER
Here, tek these, mi duck.

She presses milk and half a loaf into
starving BOY's hands.

MRS BREWSTER
Come back if you need owt else.

END SCENE.

13

You get the picture.

Living here, you're not likely to get invited round for a cup of Earl Grey and a cucumber sandwich too often, but people still care about each other.

My mum took off with another bloke eleven years ago when I was still at nursery school. I can't remember her at all, although I know Dad's got a few photos put away somewhere.

I think that might be something I could put in my journal that Freya would find interesting. Counsellors like that sort of thing.

I've not told anybody this, but I dream about Mum now and then. She's just a presence rather than a person. A clean scent like soap or wash powder, a softness on my cheek.

Sometimes I wake up crying, but I never remember her face.

There's no way I'm writing any of that down; it sounds like one of those reality-TV sob stories. I don't want Freya thinking I'm soft.

So, maybe I could write about Dad.

My dad leaves a lot to be desired when it comes to parenting, but he's raised me – well, more like dragged me up – all on his own since Mum left.

We stick together, me and my dad. So far, we've managed to get by.

2

I go to Wells Road Comprehensive School.

It's a couple of miles away from our flat, but I save the bus money Dad gives me and walk to school every day. It comes in handy when he's away from home for longer and I run out of food money.

After school I sometimes go for a longer walk to clear my head. One of my favourite places is right here, down by the canal. I've come down here instead of going straight home because it beats sitting in a cold, empty flat.

I walk past a couple of fishermen nestled close to their olive-green dome tents and keep going until I get to my favourite wooden bench that sits on a patch of grass in a quiet spot overlooking the canal.

I look up to Nottingham Castle perched high on a rock, surveying the city. It looks like it could tip right off in a strong wind, but I'm not fooled. It's been there, solid and imposing, since the seventeenth century, and it'll probably still be there in another four hundred years.

When Grandad was alive, we'd cycle all over the city, up and down the canal paths. Past Castle Wharf, where the waterside bars and restaurants stand smartly in line, glitzy and ostentatious alongside the tired, disused warehouses that crumble into the water like brittle old bones.

Grandad showed me where the old Raleigh factory used to be on Triumph Road. He worked there for forty-three years.

'Nottingham once made the finest cycles in the world but the boggers sold it all off,' Grandad would rant in his broad Nottingham accent on a regular basis. 'Like they sold out on the pits and everything else that gave ordinary folks a decent living.'

We'd park our bikes up and sit by the canal and he'd pipe down a bit while we ate our corned-beef and beetroot sandwiches.

The longboats chugged past, leaving a trail of frothy black water and diesel fumes in their wake, and Grandad would fall quiet then, his eyes sort of fading out as if someone had twisted a dimmer switch behind them.

He had loads of stories about 'the good old days' as he used to call them. He could remember every detail about what he got up to as a lad, things that happened when he worked in the Raleigh factory, and the holidays in Cornwall him and Gran used to have before she died. But then he'd often forget what happened yesterday or just last week.

I wish I'd have listened a bit closer to Grandad's stories now. Some of them would make brilliant screenplays.

After we'd sat by the canal a while, he'd spark back to

life and we'd be off, cycling home again.

Grandad's bike was mint: a top-of-the-range Raleigh Chopper that he'd helped manufacture with his own hands.

I don't know what happened to our cycles. I think they must've just got chucked out when the council's Housing Department cleared his council house.

'Penny for them?'

I snap out of my memories to see a girl about my age standing over me with her hands on her hips. 'I've been standing here for the last half an hour and you didn't even know, you numpty.'

I've only been sitting on the bench for ten minutes, so I doubt that.

Her southern accent sounds bold and cheeky. She's wearing cut-off denim shorts and a T-shirt that looks at least a size too small and shows her midriff. I look away.

'Not very talkative, are you?' She sits down on the bench next to me.

I don't want to look at her, but she's staring so hard. Part of me doesn't want to be rude and part of me doesn't want to look soft. So I stare back.

Her skin is the colour of pale coffee, and her thick, curly black hair is tied up with red-and-white-spotted ribbon into two fizzy bunches that remind me of Minnie Mouse and make me smile.

'What's so funny?' She wrinkles her nose and I spot a

17

fine spattering of freckles that radiate out to her cheeks.

'Nothing,' I say with a shrug, feeling a heat in my cheeks.

'We got off on the wrong foot, didn't we? I'm Amelia.' She holds out her hand and when I reach for it, she snatches it back and laughs like a drain.

Her front tooth is chipped and the others look a bit crooked, but they're very white. 'Sorry, the handshake thing is my favourite trick.'

I look away, out across the greasy black swell of the canal. I can tell by the colour of the water that rain might be coming soon.

'So, what's your name then?'

'Calum,' I murmur, keeping my eyes on the water.

'Folks aren't very friendly around here, are they?'

'Probably not if you trick them and call them numpties.'

I scowl, and she claps her hands with delight.

'Doesn't take much to say hello though, does it?' She taps me on the arm. 'Want to see our boat? We're moored just down there.' She nods past the bend in the canal. 'It's a narrowboat.'

I've always wanted to have a look inside a proper narrowboat like the ones you see chugging up and down the Trent, but I don't want to encourage Amelia. She's so full-on and confident, she sets my teeth on edge.

'Come on, we're not a family of vampires, honest. There's just me, my little brother and my mum.'

'OK,' I hear myself say, and I stand up.

'It's just down here.' She slips in front of me and moves quickly ahead on strong, striding legs. She's wearing battered Converse trainers.

'Do you live around here?' I say to her back.

'Nah, we're from just outside London originally. We go all over the place though.' She turns round and grins at me, walking backwards without slowing down. 'Never been to Nottingham before. Probably won't come again, if everyone's as miserable as you.'

'Thanks.'

'Only joking, mate. Have a laugh.'

She says 'laugh' like 'larrf'. She's about halfway between being irritating and fascinating.

'It's just here, round this bend.'

We walk a few more steps and a glossy red-and-blue-painted narrowboat comes into view.

'There she is: *My Fair Lady*. That's her name, see.'

Plants and flowers in misshapen, brightly painted china pots clutter and spill from the top of the boat. A man in navy dungarees bends over, prodding at something mechanical with a spanner.

'Ma!' Amelia calls, waving both arms in the air.

The man stands up and steps off the boat, wiping his hands on an oily rag. Except when we get closer, I see that the man is a woman. Must be Amelia's mum.

'There you are, love; wondered where you got to.

Found a new friend, have you?'

I feel my cheeks heat up. Amelia turns to look at me and laughs.

'I don't think he's made his mind up yet so don't scare him off.'

Amelia's mum runs her hand through her dark blonde cropped hair and sticks out a grubby hand. 'I'm Sandy.'

I move to shake her hand and she snatches it away.

'Sorry, I can't help it,' she says, grinning. 'One of my favourite tricks, that one.'

I wait until they've finished laughing.

Fifteen minutes ago I was sitting quietly on a bench, thinking about the good times I had down here with Grandad, and now somehow I've ended up stuck with these two jokers.

'His name's Calum,' Amelia says. 'He wants to look at the boat.'

'She asked me to,' I say quickly. Amelia is making it sound like it was all my idea.

'No worries.' Sandy grins. She's got the same shower of freckles on her lightly tanned face as Amelia. 'But I've got this generator dismantled now, so come back tomorrow, Calum, and Amelia will show you round then, OK, love?'

I glance at what look like engine parts, spread all over the front of the boat behind Sandy.

'Will you come back down tomorrow, Calum?' Amelia

steps in front of me so I can't move. 'Promise?'

'OK.' I nod.

She steps aside and watches me walk away. When I get to the bend in the canal, I look back. It feels like I've had a lucky escape.

Amelia is still watching. She waves, but I don't wave back.

3

Most people would probably be glad they've got a day off, even if it's because they've been excluded. But I'd rather be at school.

I never get any hassle there because nobody messes with Linford and Jack, not if they want to keep their teeth.

School is warm and I get a hot meal every lunchtime. Plus, I get to hang around at the edges of the action and watch what the others get up to.

Being stuck in lessons beats dashing to the corner shop at eleven o'clock at night to top up the electricity meter card when the lights go out. Or poking a metal coat hanger down the drain to unblock the shower for the hundredth time.

Sometimes there's stuff to do that won't wait until Dad gets back.

He works all over the place – up north, down south and, since Christmas, he's even been going across to Poland once a fortnight.

I bet you're wondering what Dad does for a living. Well join the club, because even I'm not sure. I used to question him about it but he'd just wink and say, 'If anybody asks, just tell them I'm in imports and exports.'

Sometimes, if he's back home for more than a couple of days, he takes on handyman jobs locally, but that doesn't happen too often because he's back and forth so much.

These days I don't bother asking questions; I just wait for him to come back. He tries to make up for being away so much then. He takes me out for a pizza, or sometimes we order a takeaway and watch the footie.

When he's home for two or three days, he starts trying to lay down the law and it bugs me that I'm supposed to just flip back to being a kid again.

'Get your room cleared up; it's a doss-hole.'

'This whole flipping flat's a doss-hole, haven't you noticed?'

'Don't give me that lip, remember who the gaffer is around here.'

Yeah, right. Until the next time 'the gaffer' goes on a job again. Then I'll be back to playing Mr Fix-It again, whether I like it or not.

'Don't say nothing about nothing to nobody,' Dad always warns me before he leaves for his next job. 'We don't need other people sticking their noses into our business; we can cope just fine on our own.'

Or at least that's what he used to say, before everything changed.

Before those two turned up and ruined everything.

But I'll get to that later.

23

*

I make myself beans on toast for lunch and watch a bit of TV, but by two o'clock I'm bored out of my skull.

I keep thinking about Amelia and her narrowboat.

I promised her I'd go back but I probably won't. She's irritating and, anyway, what would my mates say if they found out I'd been hanging around with a girl?

I could just go for a walk though, I reason with myself.

Anyway, why should I stop going down the canal just in case Amelia's on the prowl? I've lived here for years, which gives me more right. She just got here. Besides, she's probably not in, if her mum has already got her into a local school.

I'm not usually around in the middle of the afternoon and the canal path is quiet today – even the fishermen are scarce. One or two cyclists zip by and an old man and his equally old dog both dodder past me, but apart from that, it's peaceful and serene.

I sit on a bench and watch the water ebb and flow for a bit, but my insides feel itchy, like I'm full of marching soldier ants and it's hard to sit still for very long.

I decide to have a walk down and see if *My Fair Lady* is still moored past the bend. Just in case she's in, I could knock on the door, if that's even what you're supposed to do with boats. Then again, I probably won't knock. I don't want Amelia thinking I'm desperate to be her friend or that I *like* her or something.

The air is warmer and dryer than yesterday, and the water, although still deep and dark, doesn't seem quite as dense and oily today.

'You came back!'

I turn round to find Amelia and Sandy walking up behind me, carrying bags of what looks like food shopping. A wide grin spreads on Amelia's face.

I stop walking and stick my hands into my jeans pockets, kicking at the dirt path. My heart starts to thud.

'No school today, Calum?' Sandy asks as they draw level with me.

'No, I . . .' I don't want Amelia's mum to get the wrong impression so I stretch the truth a bit. 'There's a staff training day today.'

'In the middle of the week? That's unusual.' Amelia grins at me and I look away.

I could ask her the same question. Surely *she* should be in school if they're staying here? I offer to carry one of the heaviest bags instead and Sandy lets me.

We set off walking again and soon the boat comes into view.

'There she is,' Amelia sings. 'The prettiest narrowboat in the land.'

They both have this weird habit of talking about the boat like it's a living thing.

I can't deny it *is* eye-catching. The main body of the boat is painted in a glossy, deep racing green with blue sills and bright red trims. Loads of bright, strong colours together ought to be too much, but somehow it works.

Dad would call it 'gaudy'.

'Thanks for helping us lug the supplies back,' Sandy says. 'Do you want to stay for some tea, love?'

'Oh go on, Calum,' Amelia pleads. 'Ma's making her spicy vegetable tagine. It's awesome. And you can meet Spike and—'

'Give the lad a chance to reply!' Sandy laughs.

'OK.' I shrug, feeling my cheeks start to burn again. 'Thanks.'

Thick ropes tether the boat to the rusting iron mooring rings dotted along the bank. *My Fair Lady* seems to shudder a little on the water as we approach her, as if she knows we're there.

Sandy clambers on first, dumps the bags on deck and reaches her hands out to take our bags.

'Come on.' Amelia jumps on to the boat next and I follow her. I can feel the subtle movement of the water in my stomach but *My Fair Lady* feels solid and reliable under my feet.

'Welcome aboard, Calum. Go and have a look around, love,' Sandy says.

Inside, the boat is long and narrow, as I expected. It is warm and feels friendly and cosy.

'Here she is.' Amelia wafts her hand around. 'This is home.'

Every inch of available space on the walls is filled with *something*. There are both useful and decorative objects hanging or stacked together. White nets at the windows give privacy from the towpath, and orange-and-purple-checked curtains add even more colour.

At the far end of the boat, a black cast-iron wood-burner dominates the inside space; red-hot embers glow through the sooty glass panel.

The kitchen area is tiny, its wooden cupboards painted in mint green. Shelves piled high with mismatched crockery are partly hidden by a checked curtain.

'On a boat you call it the *galley*, not the kitchen,' Amelia tells me.

Floral mugs in different colours and shapes hang higgledy-piggledy from a row of brass hooks under the wall cupboards, and a cobalt blue kettle gives off a low whistle as it simmers on the back burner of a gas hob.

Amelia opens the little fridge and pours us two glasses of readymade strawberry milkshake.

'Let's go and sit down,' she says.

We take the drinks to the other end of the boat near the wood-burner. A long, thin couch runs along one wall and is piled up with patchwork blankets and cushions. It feels like I'm sitting on a squashy beanbag.

'So, are you here on holiday?' I ask, slurping the

milkshake and savouring the sharp tang of strawberry on my tongue. 'I mean, where do you actually live?'

'You don't get it, do you?' Amelia grins. 'We live on *My Fair Lady*. We live in lots of different places.'

I frown, trying to get my head around it.

She points to a decorative plaque above her head: *Home is where one starts from.*

'That's a T. S. Eliot quote. It means home is anywhere you want it to be, I suppose. It doesn't have to be in one set place.' She scowls at my blank face. 'You know who T. S. Eliot is, right?'

'Yeah.' I shrug. 'Sort of.'

She grins. 'He was a poet and a playwright.'

'Right. So, if you're living all over the place, which school do you go to?'

'Ma homeschools us,' she says matter-of-factly. 'Me and Spike. The lady on the boat next door is watching him while me and Ma popped to the shop.'

The small door at the other end of the boat slides open and a small, wiry boy of about seven bounces towards us, barefoot and dressed only in a pair of shorts.

'Calum, meet my brother, Spike.'

'Hello,' I say, keeping my hands firmly around my glass. I'm not going to fall for the handshake trick a third time.

'Is this your boyfriend, Mimi?' The lad looks me up and down.

'No!' I feel my face flood with colour.

'Just a mate.' Amelia grins. 'Cheeky little rat. Say hello.'

'Hello,' Spike says. He sits down next to me, too close. I want to inch a bit further along but he fixes me with the brightest emerald green eyes I've ever seen and I can't look away.

His dark blond hair is long and hangs raggedly on his shoulders. He's got this outdoorsy smell about him – not dirty, just fresh and energetic. If energetic even has a smell.

'So, as I was saying, Ma homeschools us and we travel around the country. We never stay anywhere longer than two weeks.'

'Why not?'

'Cos Ma's only got a short-term licence. We have to keep moving. It's the *law*, don't you know.' Amelia screws up her nose.

'So you can't just moor up and live in one place?'

'Not unless we get a residential licence, and they're in very short supply, hardly anybody gets them. The authorities think they own the water, the sky, the air we breathe. We have to ask if we can stay here because it supposedly all belongs to them.' Amelia has stopped looking mischievous and now her brown eyes are big and serious. 'How can that be right?'

4

By the end of the week we've all served our exclusion time and it is business as usual back at school.

Mr Fox announces we have a special Friday whole school assembly. Everyone shuffles into the hall and the noise level rises as we all discuss what it might be about.

'I'm pleased and proud to introduce a very special guest,' he beams from the front. 'My talented son Hugo.'

We all groan. Mr Fox wheels his 'talented son Hugo' into school at least once a term to tell us what a wonderfully good actor he is and how we can all aspire to be like him, even though we're so obviously poor with few prospects.

'Wake me up when he's finished yacking,' Jack says with a yawn.

'I'm here today to tell you that my success is nothing to do with privilege.' Hugo strides up and down at the front of the hall. He's warming to the task now and gesticulating wildly with his arms. 'I'm a respected local young actor because I've worked hard.' Mr Fox stands next to him like a nodding dog. 'Some of *you* could achieve too, if you're willing to persevere. Though I do appreciate that living around here on the estate, success must sometimes seem a million miles away.'

With the expressions on their faces, one or two of the teachers look as if they're sick to death of listening to Hugo Fox, too.

'I'm lucky enough to go to a private drama school in the city,' he drones on. 'But you have great facilities right here on the estate, and I have some very exciting news to announce.' He stops talking for a moment and I almost expect there to be a drum roll. 'I'm going to be running some free drama workshops at the Expressions community centre. We might even be able to get some real actors and film directors in to speak to students—'

'Hugo is very kindly giving his time to help young people in disadvantaged areas,' Mr Fox interrupted, beaming at his son. 'I would encourage you all to take advantage of this.'

'Young people like you,' Hugo declares, throwing his hands out to us. 'You can work towards a better life right now.'

It all sounds like a cheesy advert on the telly.

But film directors coming in to speak to us . . . now that might be interesting. If only they thought we really had a chance.

★

INT. EXPRESSIONS COMMUNITY CENTRE – SATURDAY
AFTERNOON
Young people from the local area are gathered,

listening to a famous film DIRECTOR speak.

DIRECTOR
(*enthusiastic*)
So, let's talk about job goals. There are
lots of different jobs in the film industry.
Roadies, acting extras, catering staff, hair
and make-up; you get the idea. Anyone here
interested in working in the industry?

Nobody raises a hand. DIRECTOR scans crowd,
his eyes settling on a BOY. He points at
him.

DIRECTOR
You there. What do *you* want to do with your
life?

Everyone turns to look at the BOY. BOY's
face reddens. He looks at his hands and
stays silent.

DIRECTOR
Come on, don't be shy. Everyone has dreams,
what's yours?

                            BOY
                        (*nervously*)
            I want to write screenplays.

BOY thinks he sees a tiny smirk play around
DIRECTOR's lips.

                          DIRECTOR
                     (*winking at crowd*)
              Did you say 'screenplays'?

                            BOY
     Yes. Screenplays for movies. Movies with big
                budgets and top actors.

There is a faint ripple of laughter behind
him.

                          DIRECTOR
              And where do you live, boy?

                            BOY
            I live here, on the estate.

                          DIRECTOR
        And have you ever been to Hollywood?

BOY

No.

DIRECTOR

And do you know anyone in the industry, any
screenwriters or contacts that can give you
a break?

BOY

No.

DIRECTOR

And are your parents sending you to drama
school?

BOY

No.

DIRECTOR

Well, all I can say then is good luck with
that one.

DIRECTOR throws back his head and bursts out
laughing.

Loud, roaring laughter erupts from the
crowd. Laughing residents from the estate

34

gather at the open doors. The BOY spots his own dad at the back. He's wiping his eyes and laughing.

The sound of laughter is deafening.

BOY slopes away, pushes his way out of the crowd and leaves the building.

END SCENE.

I force my attention back to the room.

'So, is anyone here interested in coming along?' Hugo asks. 'I'll be taking names at the end and you'll be guaranteed a place.'

A few hands are cautiously raised. I tuck my own hands under my thighs, the cruel laughter from my imagined scene still ringing in my ears.

Despite Mr Fox's enthusiastic thanks to his son and trying to get us whipped up into a frenzy of admiration, there is only a smattering of applause from the teachers at the end of Hugo's talk.

After the last lesson of the morning we meet as usual outside the Technology block, before walking across the courtyard for lunch.

I'm last to get there and when I follow the lads inside

the building, Linford hangs back in the corridor outside the bustling dinner hall. He slings an arm across my shoulders and I sag a little under the pressing weight.

'You're not planning on going to see that counsellor like Mr Fox suggested, are you, mate?'

I swallow hard.

The others overhear and stop walking to listen.

Jack's mouth drops open. 'You're not going to see her, are you, Cal?'

'Course not.' I shrug.

Linford gives a little shake of his head. 'Course he's not. I'm just making sure, after the Sly Old Fox tried to get us all to agree to it.'

I wish he'd take his arm away. He's taller and broader than me and his elbow is digging into the middle of my back. But he tightens his grip.

'A little bird tells me you were over in the Admin block this morning.' Linford's grin fades a bit.

'I saw you walk over there, Cal,' Harry says apologetically. 'But like I told Linford, there's no way you'd be going to see that poxy counsellor.'

He means without clearing it with Linford first.

I get this feeling inside that reminds me of when I was a little kid and I'd done something wrong without realizing what.

'I had to go over there to the school office to get a contact form to change my dad's mobile number, that's all.' I shrug as if I don't know what the big deal is. 'I thought Mr Fox said we'd all got to go to see the counsellor, though.'

'Did he? I thought he'd just *suggested* it.' Linford pulls a cartoon frown at the others. 'The Sly Old Fox says we should do a lot of things, but we usually ignore him – right, lads?'

Jack and Harry nod their approval.

'I just thought I'd ask, Cal, because that would be bang out of order, mate. If I found out you'd been to see her, I mean.'

I think about my chat with Freya, how she said it was just between the two of us.

'No worries.' I drop my head forward and try to shrug him off, but he still doesn't move his arm.

'They'd love it if they got us grassing each other up. That's why the Fox wants us all to go.' Linford's face hardens. 'She'll start off all friendly, get you to write a load of stuff down, and then turn it against you. Turn it against *us*.'

'Yeah, I know,' I say, sensing a damp patch forming at the bottom of my back.

At last, Linford's arm slides off my shoulders and his lips peel back revealing two rows of neat teeth.

'Cool. I knew you wouldn't be so stupid.'

The back of my neck prickles.

We're still standing in the corridor outside the dinner

hall looking at each other. Someone has pulled the outer door shut and the air hangs around us, heavy and warm.

Linford smiles then and the other lads grin. We all start walking towards the double doors of the dinner hall and finally I feel my shoulders drop a little.

I pull open the door and a flood of noise billows out like escaping steam. I turn to look back at Linford and a brief shadow flits across his eyes, like something glossy and dark swarming underwater.

The dinner hall is heaving, but our table remains unoccupied in the far back corner.

We collect our loaded food trays and walk through the bustling tables. Linford leads the way and chair legs scrape the floor as other students shuffle hastily aside to let him through.

We're nearly at our seats when he suddenly stops walking and spins round, his face animated and split into a wide grin.

'Watch this.'

He stops at a table where three girls sit huddled together over their food at one end. At the other end, sitting alone, is the new boy who got us all excluded.

He picks at his food with his head down, frayed blazer sleeves trailing down his fingers.

Linford kicks the leg of his chair hard.

The boy visibly jumps and his head jerks up. He opens

his mouth to say something but swallows it back down when he sees Linford.

'All right, Immi? That's your name, isn't it? Immi Grant?'

The boy looks down at his food.

'Maybe that should be *Ignorant*, not Immigrant,' Jack hisses.

Linford's eyes scan the hall but the lunchtime supervisors are all busy up front, sorting out the unruly queue.

'When someone asks you a question in this country, Immi, you're supposed to answer.'

'Yeah, it's what we call *manners*,' Jack adds.

The girls have stopped eating and the people seated at nearby tables are now watching with interest.

'I'll ask you again,' Linford repeats. 'You all right, Immi Grant?'

Snorts of laughter roll at us like a wave from surrounding tables.

'My name is Sergei Zurakowski,' the boy says quietly, his eyes cast down at his plate.

'Flipping heck, that's a bit of a mouthful.' Linford screws his face up in distaste.

'I am named after my mother's father, who was Russian.'

Sergei is misunderstanding. He thinks Linford is actually interested in his name.

'Yeah, well, enough of the boring family history. I think we'd better just stick with Immi.'

'Sounds good to me,' Jack agrees.

Sergei's long skinny legs are folded awkwardly under the table. His trouser hems are ragged and the toes of his shoes scuffed to a dirty grey against the dull black leather. One of his feet jiggles up and down as if there's music playing in his head.

'Linford, I think one of the dinner ladies is on her way over,' I call. He never knows when to stop.

Jack glances up the hall.

'Nah, they're all busy, Cal, stop worrying.'

'I'm glad to see you're enjoying your free English nosh, Immi,' Linford continues pleasantly, as if he's discussing the weather. 'And I'm pleased you're getting your free education, courtesy of the British taxpayers.' His eyes flash dangerously. 'Why don't you have some free water, too?'

Linford upends his full glass over Sergei's meal tray and water gushes down, flooding his food. He shakes out the last few drops for good measure.

Sergei doesn't jump back or cry out in surprise. He stares down at his ruined food and he doesn't move at all.

A roar of shocked laughter rises all around us and Linford walks quickly away. I hear the dinner staff calling for calm from over the other side of the room, but by this time we're already sitting innocently at our table.

'Plans for Friday night then, lads?' Linford announces when we sit down with our trays – as if nothing's happened. 'My old fella's got me and him tickets for Forest's home game. What's everybody else up to?'

'Cinema with my brother and his mates,' Harry mumbles through a mouthful of food. 'Don't know what film we're seeing yet though.'

'We've got a houseful. Aunties, uncles, cousins. Flipping nightmare.' Jack rolls his eyes. 'It's Mum's birthday, so at least I should be able to smuggle a couple of beers up to my room.'

'Cool.' Linford grins.

I glance over at Sergei. He's trying to roll up his sopping blazer sleeves while the people around him stare on.

'Cal?' Linford looks over at Sergei and then back at me. 'I asked what you're up to tonight?'

Something usually pops into my head if anyone asks, but today I can't think – I've got brain freeze. The sounds of cutlery chinking and plates rattling grows louder in my ears but there is still no answer for Linford.

Harry and Jack look up from their food.

'He's been struck dumb.' Jack smirks, shovelling in a forkful of pasta.

'Bowling,' I finally manage. 'Me and Dad are going ten-pin bowling tonight.'

Linford nods slowly, his dark eyes pinned to me.

I look down and push my food around. The spaghetti looks like a tangle of worms on my plate.

Out of the corner of my eye, I see Sergei stand up and leave the dinner hall.

I put down my fork. I don't feel hungry any more.

5

My mates get off home as soon as school finishes so they are on time for their families and the stuff they have planned.

If Dad was home we could talk about our day and talk about what we might do at the weekend. But this morning he texted to say he won't be back until tomorrow night, or it might even be Sunday if the job needs him to stay longer.

I'm not sure what I'll do all weekend.

I decide to walk the long way home, up St Ann's Well Road and back down Woodborough Road, the steep hill that leads into the back roads of our estate. It's really warm and fine out. For the first time it really feels like summer is here to stay.

There are loads of little kids scuttling around, having just been collected from the nearby primary school by their parents. Some squeal and yell, running round like they just escaped prison, but most walk nicely hand in hand with their mum or dad, the kids relaying their day at school. Looking up at the adults like they are their whole world.

A few more years and they'll drop into the real world,

realize they're on their own.

In a week's time, all the schools break up for their six weeks of summer and then it will be much quieter around here at this time of day. I've been trying not to think about the summer, about what I'm going to do every day, but you know what happens when you try not to think of something. Suddenly it's all you can think about.

I've had a cool idea bouncing around my head for a few days. I've been thinking that maybe I could convince Dad to take me with him on a couple of jobs, so I can see what he really does for a living.

It might be interesting and I could properly help him out so he can see I'm not a kid any more. I could see some different places and I'd be able to spend time with Dad instead of being on my own in the flat for days on end.

All I have to do is pick the right time to ask him, and to do that, he needs to be home. I dig into my pocket and peer at the scant pile of coins in my hand. Three pounds and eighty-two pence. No chance of a takeaway pizza tonight then.

There's half a pint of milk, a yogurt and an egg in the fridge. Plus six slices of white bread with a few dots of green on, which doesn't bother me because I'll be toasting it anyway. And mould is only penicillin, so it won't kill me.

I reach the top of St Ann's Well Road and the steepness levels off at last, bending to the left on to Mapperley Top.

44

I glance across at the big gated houses, wondering who they are trying to keep out and whether it feels different to wake up and go to bed at night when you live in a place like that. The air seems clearer up here, the sky bluer. Our flat is only about half a mile away at the bottom of the hill, but it feels like a whole world apart.

I walk for another ten minutes and just before I turn into the estate, I pass the Expressions community building across the road. Built last year from European funding, the brickwork glows a vibrant terracotta in the sunlight.

This is where Hugo Fox is going to be running his workshops, where film directors will come and talk to us no-hopers.

The gates are closed and locked now, but it will be opening up soon for the Friday evening activities they run.

Last week, the manager rang Dad to pop over and secure an outside door after an attempted break-in. Some people just can't bear to see anything new and nice around here.

'Arty types with more money than sense,' Dad always says.

Mr Rhodes, the drama teacher, took us down for a look at the start of the spring term. Inside it still smells new and the toilets are clean with no wee on the floor or graffiti on the walls.

I've never been to any of their workshops but I like the newness of the building. It feels like someone important remembered our shoddy estate was tucked away back here and still thought we were worth investing in. It's a cool place to hang out, nobody bothers you, and you can watch the activities even if you don't want to take part. It's warmer than the flat in the winter months, too.

Since I walked to school this morning, something has been attached to the railings of the gates. A poster, or something similar, is encased in a plastic sleeve to protect it against the weather.

I cross over the road and take a quick look round before I stop to read the sheet. I don't want word getting back to the lads I'm interested in doing a daft drama class or something else they'd think is naff.

When I see the sheet's printed headline, I freeze.

The traffic sounds from the main road, the birds tweeting in the trees, and even the bus that passes me full of tired-looking passengers – everything fades into the background.

SEND US YOUR SCRIPT!

A lingering buzz travels from the top of my head right down to my big toes.

My eyes scan the poster, picking out the main bits.

Happily we have secured European funding ... for young people working with Expressions to make a short film, set in the Mapperley, St Ann's or Dales wards. We are inviting local young people aged 13–18 to submit a screenplay on the subject: 'A Place I Want to Go' ...

I could write a screenplay and send it in! Instead of just doing it in my head, I could actually put something down on paper. But what would I write about that would be interesting enough to make a film about? All I really know about is life on the estate, and nobody is interested in *that*. St Ann's isn't a place anyone wants to go to or find out about.

The buzz is replaced by a clammy crawl that slowly covers my skin.

I enjoyed the daydream; it was nice while it lasted. Linford, Jack and Harry would fall about laughing if they knew I'd nearly been sucked in.

Entering a competition like this is just the sort of thing that *other people* do. Probably someone who lives in one of those big gated houses up on Mapperley Top. Some kid who's travelled the world and had professional training, knows how to set stuff out like a proper script. But something still makes me slide out one of the photocopies from behind the display poster, fold it up and tuck it into the side pocket of my rucksack. I might read it later, if I've nothing better to do.

Just as I'm resealing the Velcro strip on my bag, I see a quick movement out of the corner of my eye. On the other side of the building someone just dashed behind the bins, I'm sure of it.

The building itself is all locked up so I doubt it's a member of the Expressions staff. I move away from the metal swirls of the gate and walk around the side where I can see a bit clearer through the wire fencing.

There it is again, a flash of movement.

And then . . . nothing.

I stand and watch for a couple more minutes.

The road is quiet, the birdsong uninterrupted, and everything is still and undisturbed once more.

Whoever it was has found a way of disappearing.

Whoever it was doesn't want to be seen.

6

I don't turn into the estate after all. I carry on walking.

I cross over Huntingdon Street, gridlocked with after-work traffic and choked up with exhaust fumes, and keep going until I get to Mansfield Road.

I head for the bench outside the big solicitor's office on the corner and next to the Victoria Centre shopping mall.

Lots of people are swarming out of the centre, clutching bulging shopping bags. They all look happy it's the weekend, but maybe I just think that because I'm dreading it.

I sit down. One of the wooden slats on the bench is broken and it sticks up like a bone, frayed and splintered. I move to the other side, sitting in a little pool of afternoon sun that illuminates me in its warm spotlight.

When Dad is working away I come here a lot after school. I can feel the buzz of other people's lives. Everybody is too busy to notice me sitting and watching – sometimes I even pinch myself to make sure I'm not a ghost.

A double-decker trundles past. Somebody shouts and when I look up, I recognize the three jeering Year Nine lads from school. One sticks two fingers up through the open top window, and another curls his hand into a loose fist and makes a rude gesture at me.

When I do the same back, a woman with her hair pulled back in a tight bun totters by on skyscraper heels and tuts loudly.

'He did it first,' I tell her, but she sticks her nose in the air like I smell bad.

I watch an old bloke over the street shuffling up the hill. I've seen him before. He's always on his own and clutches a massive blue-and-white plastic shopping bag that's hardly got anything in it. Every so often he stops for a breather before he takes another few steps. His body is permanently bent over in a 'C' shape, even when he stands still.

I wonder what he looked like when he was younger. He might have been a soldier, stood tall with his shoulders back, striding about and giving out orders to his men.

It's weird to imagine it, but one day I'll be old like him. Like my Grandad was.

Instead of thinking about what film I'm going to watch later or counting the hours until Dad gets home, I'll be worrying about how long it's going to take me to get up that hill without breaking my scrawny neck.

It makes me feel like doing something gutsy and impulsive while I've got the chance, while I'm still young. Like, I don't know – going to the Broadmarsh bus station and just getting on a coach that's going somewhere hundreds of miles away from here, away from the estate.

If I really wanted, I could do it. I'm fourteen, not four –
nobody would ask any questions.

I haven't got enough cash on me today to buy a ticket,
but that's not the point.

Daydreaming is cool because you don't have to work
out a foolproof plan of how you're going to do stuff or
wrestle with the problems that might come up.

You can just flash-forward to the good bits.

EXT. NOTTINGHAM CITY CENTRE - DUSK
Broadmarsh Bus Centre, July. City is quiet
in the lull after work and before people
come out to the pubs and restaurants for the
night.

BOY approaches ticket office.

BOY
(*with confidence*)
Ticket to London please, one way.

TICKET CLERK peers through Perspex counter
screen at BOY.

TICKET CLERK
(*suspiciously*)

How old are you?

                    BOY
Sixteen. I'm going to visit my sick nan.

CLERK hesitates then shrugs and nods. BOY
pays twenty pounds and gets a ticket. He
turns to leave.

                TICKET CLERK
                (*calls out*)
I hope your nan gets better soon.

The bus is half empty. BOY chooses a seat at
the back and falls asleep.

CUT TO:
EXT. LONDON CITY CENTRE – MIDNIGHT
BOY stands on Tower Bridge looking down
into the River Thames. The river seems alive
with reflections of the coloured lights from
buildings on the skyline. The boy identifies
The Gherkin, The Cheesegrater, The Walkie-
Talkie and The Shard.

END SCENE.

'*Excuse me?*' A voice bellows in my ear.

I jump up from the seat to find a woman wearing a very short skirt and very long earrings standing next to me with her hands on her hips. Behind her is a pushchair.

'Blimey, you were in a proper trance there – we'll never get to the park at this rate. Our Brandon's dropped his dummy under your seat. Can you reach it?'

'Oh yeah, sorry.' I reach between my feet, pick up the dummy and hand it to her.

She gives me a funny look.

'Are you all right? You were on another planet then; are you on drugs or summat?'

I say, 'No, I was just daydreaming.'

She shakes her head and manoeuvres the pushchair ready to set off again. Little Brandon's face is smeared with chocolate ice cream.

I wonder if Mum pushed me around like that when I was a little kid, if she took me to the park and stuff.

'Have a good time on the swings,' I say to the toddler.

He holds up his half-chewed cone, waves it at me and grins.

7

When I get back on to the estate, I stop at the corner shop with my handful of coins and buy a big bottle of fizzy pop and a family-sized bar of milk chocolate.

School has a zero-tolerance policy when it comes to chips, sweets and fizzy pop. None allowed. I don't know why they think that's going to stop you eating and drinking junk food. In reality, it just makes you want it more.

I don't eat the goodies now; I take them home for later. Another five minutes and I'm turning into our street.

St Matthias Road is buzzing. Hordes of little kids are out on their bikes and scooters, and a couple of older lads are playing football, using the road as a pitch and the gateposts either side as the goals.

Mr Palmer stands on sentry duty at number seventeen, guarding his sweet-pea canes against their missed shots.

Des and Sandra and their dreadlocked mates at number eleven look proper relaxed, like they've been out in the garden all day. They've made their tiny front garden into a bit of a commune. If it's not raining, they're out there every day, sitting among the dandelions cross-legged and drinking beer out of dented cans.

They play this weird music that sounds a bit like a guitar but more twangy. Their old settee has been out there so long there are flowering weeds poking up through the seat cushions.

'Peace, man,' Des shouts when he sees me.

Dad says they give our street a bad name, smoking weed and living in a doss-hole, but I raise my hand at Des.

A bit further down at number seven, Mrs Brewster's got the barbecue going on the scrubby patch of lawn she shares with the Patels who live in the downstairs flat.

Dad says that when you barbecue meat, you're supposed to wait until the flames die down and the coals turn white, but Mrs Brewster is incinerating a row of pasty sausages in a waist-high inferno.

Her twin grandsons, Armani and Versace, are barrelling around the yard jabbing at each other with sharp sticks.

'Armony! Versays!' She screeches for them to stop and then turns to me, waving a metal spatula. 'All right, Calum?'

She whips a cigarette stub out from between her dry, wizened lips. 'Nice weather for it, eh?' The teetering ash showers the cracked concrete path as she shuffles over to the gate in her floral slippers.

Mrs Brewster frowns at the pop and the chocolate bar that are wedged under my arm.

'Plenty of sausages going if you want to stay for a bit of tea, mi duck?'

'Nah thanks – me and Dad are going bowling later.'

I try to look like someone who's looking forward to their evening, but Mrs Brewster is not an easy woman to fool.

She takes a drag of her cigarette and squints her eyes against the sun to look up the road at Dad's empty parking space.

'OK, lad, so long as you're sorted.' She leans slightly forward and peers at me, the soft loose skin of her cheeks hanging either side of her mouth like fleshy curtains. 'I'd hate to think you're stuck in that flat all alone on a fine night like this, mind.'

'I'm not,' I say quickly. 'I mean, I'm fine, thanks, Mrs Brewster.'

I let out a little chuckle to show her just how fine I am, but it slips out too high and tight, like an overstretched violin string.

Inside the cool flat, my arms prickle with goosebumps and my ears echo in the sudden silence.

I kick the door closed behind me and walk into the living room. In here, I can still hear the muted sounds from outdoors. Squealing, laughter, the hum of an occasional car offloading guests for barbecues. But stuck in here, the party atmosphere might as well be a hundred miles away.

I push the slotted blind aside and I look down on to the road. Dad's empty parking space gapes up at me like a missing tooth.

Most people are home already to enjoy the heatwave weekend that's been forecast.

I wonder briefly if I should go back down to Mrs Brewster's. I could say Dad has just texted to let me know he'll be back later now, too late to go bowling. And I can stay for a burnt sausage cob after all.

But I imagine before long she'll get round to noticing that Dad's van has actually been gone all week and she'll look at me with those X-ray boggle eyes that can detect the difference between the truth and a lie in a split-second. Mrs Brewster is wasted on looking after her grandkids; she ought to work for MI5.

Dad's constant warning about keeping our business private echoes in my ears. How if social workers and do-gooders get to hear about him working away as much, they'll cause us all sorts of problems. I could get taken into care. Dad could be prosecuted. And then where will we be?

No, it's far better if I stay on my own here in the flat with the door shut and the TV on, well away from well-meaning Mrs Brewster and her searching questions.

8

On Saturday lunchtime, I find an old instant-noodle meal at the back of the cupboard behind two rusting, out-of-date tinned peaches.

I pour the boiling water into the plastic pot and watch as the powdery noodles and lumps of tomato swell into fat, moist tapeworm and blood clots. The morsels that were probably once fresh carrots, morph into mushy orange globs like the sort that sink to the bottom of the toilet bowl when you throw up.

It sounds gross but tastes really nice, and it's definitely tons better than eating an egg on mouldy toast without any butter.

I'm a minute into the noodle waiting time when I hear the front door bang open.

My heart nearly jumps into my mouth, but then Dad barrels through, carrying his big overnight bag in one hand and clutching a couple of carrier bags full of food shopping in the other.

'You're back!'

I forget the noodles and rush over to Dad, taking the shopping bags from him before peering inside.

Pizza. Pop. Biscuits.

Result.

Dad ruffles my hair with his free hand. 'I got away a bit earlier, thought I'd surprise you.'

'Great!' I grin and start to put the shopping away.

'I'd have been here sooner but I got a call on the way home. Someone's vandalized the Expressions building again,' Dad says grimly. 'I called in on the way home to board up a couple of windows.'

I put the loaf of bread back down on the worktop and look at him.

'Do they know who's doing it?' I ask. 'The damage.'

'Probably just bored local kids, little boggers. It's sorted now anyway.' Dad shrugs. 'Any chance of a cuppa? Swine of a journey it was, another nasty accident on the M1.'

I make Dad a hot drink while he unlaces his heavy work boots and changes into his paint-spattered tracky bottoms and a T-shirt with gaping holes under the arms.

I think about telling him about the person I saw hanging around the Expressions building, but the fact was I didn't actually *see* anything. Just the shadow of a person – a movement out of the corner of my eye and then nothing.

Whoever it was had just seemed to disappear in front of my eyes.

*

Dad comes back into the sitting room, but instead of drinking his tea in front of the telly like he usually would, he sits next to me on the settee.

'Had a good week?' He takes a noisy slurp of tea and looks straight at me.

I think about what's happened. Getting a one-day exclusion and registering with the school counsellor.

''S'all right.' I shrug and leave it at that.

Dad puts his tea on the floor and sighs. He's got this stretched smile stuck to his face that looks out of place.

He picks up his mug again.

'Did *you* have a good week?' I ask, just for something to say.

'I did, lad. I did.'

Dad keeps letting out loud sighs like he's out of breath, but he can't be. He's just sitting here doing nothing.

'Are you OK, Dad?' I peer at him.

Dad squirms in his seat. His shoulders are hunched up and his face looks flushed.

'I'm fine. Couldn't be better, to tell you the truth.' He coughs and puts his mug down again. 'I'm good.'

'It's just you seem a bit, I don't know . . .' I narrow my eyes at him. 'Different.'

Dad laughs and his shoulders drop away from his ears a bit.

'Can't get anything past you, can I?' He clears his

throat and takes a breath in. 'Thing is, Cal, I've – well, I've met someone.'

'Is it about a new building project?'

This might be a good time to tell Dad about my idea to go out on a few jobs with him over the summer.

'It's not a job, no. No.' Dad's knee jiggles up and down. 'I mean, *I've met someone*. A woman.'

'A woman?' I repeat faintly.

Dad . . . and *a woman*?

I can't think of anything to say. My forehead feels hot and damp like it did just before I got chicken pox two years ago.

Dad watches me and I manage to stretch a weak smile across my face.

He shuffles to the edge of the seat cushion then and starts talking more than he's talked to me in a year. At least, it feels that way.

'She's a bit younger than me, but then age is just a number, isn't it? She's brilliant, Cal. Beautiful, bright, funny, she's everything I never thought I'd have again, after – well, you know.'

Mum.

'I wanted to tell you because Angie – that's her name – well, she's dying to come over. She says she wants to meet this brilliant son I've told her all about.'

I get a tight feeling across my chest and back like when I had to wear a rented suit for Dad's best mate's wedding.

Dad is still talking but I've stopped listening – I just watch him instead. He looks alive and energetic in a way I've never seen before. I just need to get rid of this lump in my throat and say something to show I'm happy for him.

When it all sinks in, I know I'll feel happy for him.

Dad slaps his hand down on my shoulder. A splash of tea escapes his mug and scalds my thigh through my jeans.

'Me and you, lad, we're like this –' He makes a fist in front of my face to show me just how tight we are. 'Nothing could ever come between us. You know that, don't you?'

I nod and the lump in my throat dislodges a bit but then settles itself a bit higher up.

I don't see that much of Dad for the rest of the weekend.

He paints his bedroom on Saturday afternoon and then goes out early on Sunday buying new towels and bedding and getting a load of posh food and booze in while I tidy round the flat.

Usually when he gets home, Dad puts his phone on charge in the kitchen and leaves it there all weekend. But all weekend, his phone dings every few minutes with incoming texts, and every time I look at him, if he's not reading them, he's sending his own messages.

'Angie's coming over tomorrow night,' Dad announces

at Sunday teatime, when he finally sits down to watch the match with me. 'We can all have a nice meal together.'

Maybe it's not such a bad thing after all, this Angie being around. If Dad intends keeping the cupboards and fridge stocked up.

'Can we open that carrot cake you bought tonight?' I smack my lips together, imagining the moist, spiced sponge and the buttercream icing.

'Let's wait till Angie gets here, shall we?' Dad pulls his eyes away from the telly and looks at me as if he's going to say something else, but then his eyes flick back to the game.

After a bit he winks and says, 'Angie's bringing someone with her. I think you'll enjoy getting to know him; in fact I'm certain of it. You two could even become great friends.'

I reckon she's got a dog, but he's keeping me guessing. I've always wanted one but Dad says it wouldn't be fair on an animal, stuck in the flat all day while I'm out at school and he's working away all week.

'Oh yeah, what's his name, this *someone*?' I grin, playing along.

'You'll find out when you meet him tomorrow.' Dad takes a swig from his beer can. 'It'll be a nice surprise.'

9

Mid-morning on Monday, I have a counselling appointment with Freya.

If you have a 'pastoral appointment' – that's what they call stuff like counselling sessions – you're allowed to miss part of your lesson to attend.

Luckily for me I get to skive off most of double maths, and even better, all my mates are in a lower set and in other lessons. So it should be easy to slip into Freya's office unnoticed.

I think about Linford's disapproving comments and how he was adamant none of us should see the counsellor without him saying so. He reckons Freya is out to get us and can't be trusted.

Sometimes it feels like he's the adult and that me, Jack and Harry are just little kids for him to order about. It never used to be like that. Once, we were all on the same level, but at some point, Linford put himself in charge without any of us noticing.

Now it feels impossible to do anything about it.

I can't just not turn up for my counselling appointment today, so I'll have to go for this one last session and then tell Freya that I can't come any more. I've got no choice;

it's more than my life's worth if Linford finds out I'm talking to her behind his back.

I walk across the inner courtyard to Freya's office in the Admin block. The sun throws shadows on to the smooth new flagstones the school had laid during spring half-term. The paving is arranged in alternate diamond shapes of cream and pale salmon. There are no blots of chewing gum or foaming mounds of gob decorating the new area yet.

It reminds me that Dad was supposed to lay a little patio on our bit of scrubby lawn outside. At first, he said he'd do it in April, then it got deferred to May. And then he had the chance of doing some well-paid work in Poland, so he reckoned he'd definitely be able to get it sorted by June. He said we might even get a small barbecue set up on there, too. Fat chance. It's already mid-July now and we're breaking up from school next week. Still no patio.

I curl my fingers around my new notebook in my blazer pocket. Freya asked me to bring it with me for my next session.

I thought I'd be full of dread at the thought of having to talk to her again but, weirdly, I feel a bit lighter inside. As if some of the dark shadows have been driven away.

When I approach Freya's office door, my heart starts to race. I knock and wait, like the sign says.

The door springs open and I step back as another

student emerges from her office. It's Sergei Zurakowski. He holds the door open for me as he steps out into the corridor. I feel him watching me but I don't meet his eyes.

Freya's bright freckled face and shock of short red hair appears in front of me.

'See you next time, Sergei,' she calls to his back before closing the door behind us. 'Good morning, Calum.'

'Morning,' I mumble and shuffle into her office, standing uselessly in the middle of the room. What was Sergei Zurakowski doing in here? And what's he been saying to Freya?

'Sit anywhere you like.' She nods towards the upholstered seats.

I shrug off my rucksack and sink down into the chair that's furthest away from her. I stare at the water jug and two glasses that sit on the low table in front of us.

'So –' Freya picks up the jug – 'how have you been, Calum, had a good weekend?'

I watch as the sparkling water tinkles into both glasses. I shrug. ''S'all right.'

'Looking forward to the summer holidays?'

I shrug again. I don't want to think about being stuck in the flat on my own all day for six long weeks.

'We can fit in one more session on Friday before we break up if you like?' Freya smiles. 'And through the summer, if you're around, I do weekly sessions at the

Expressions community centre on the estate.'

I give a quick nod. At the end of my appointment, I'll tell her I'm not coming any more.

'Did you manage to write anything in your notebook?' Freya asks.

I delve into my inside blazer pocket and pull out the notebook, sliding it across the table towards her.

'I don't know if I've done it right,' I mutter.

She shakes her head and pushes the notebook back towards me.

'It's *your* notebook, Calum. If you want to, you can open it and read out what you've written. But that's your choice.'

Strange. Linford said her job was to vet every word, to try and catch us out.

'Like I said before,' Freya continues, 'it's not homework. You're not being tested in any way, OK?'

I nod.

'You can relax. There is no right or wrong way to do this.'

I look at her but my mouth feels dry and I can't think of what to say.

'So . . .' She beams and takes a sip of water. 'What did you manage to get down?'

I take a big gulp of my own water and open the notebook.

'I wrote a list of things I like doing in my spare time.'

I feel a rush of heat in my cheeks. 'Just stupid stuff.'

Freya sits back, folds her pale, freckled hands into her lap and waits.

I stare at my own scrawl on the first page. Why did I even bother writing this drivel?

'*Stuff I like doing.*' I read out the heading and wish more than anything I could dig a deep hole right now and jump in it. '*Number one. Watching films.*'

'Well, would you know it, a man after my own heart!' Freya sings in her lilting accent. 'What kind of films?'

'Dunno, all sorts.' I shuffle in my seat but I can't seem to get comfy. 'I like action films. And sci-fi, I suppose.'

'OK, have you watched any independent films at all?'

I shake my head. I don't know what she means.

'It's my favourite genre of film,' she says. 'Carry on.'

I look at the next thing on my list and I feel my cheeks burn harder.

'*Number two. Writing screenplays.*'

I waft the edges of my blazer a bit. The room didn't seem this hot when I first came in.

'You write screenplays? Why, that's just fantastic, Calum.'

I glance over at her to see if she's smirking at the thought of someone like me writing a script, but she isn't. Smirking, I mean. She actually looks impressed.

'They're not like proper plays or anything,' I say quickly. 'I mean, they're not very good.'

68

'Have you got one with you?' Freya leans forward. 'A screenplay you wrote that you can let me read?'

'No,' I say.

'Are you in a writers group or anything?'

I have to smile. She must think I'm some kind of professional writer or something.

'Why is that funny, Calum?'

'There's nothing like that round here, and anyway, I don't write proper screenplays like in the films. Mostly I just do it in my head. That's why I'm not entering the Expressions competition.'

She throws me a puzzled look and I remember the flyer in my rucksack. I pull it out of the side pocket and hand it to her.

'But this would be perfect,' she breathes when she opens it up. 'I mean, this is a fantastic opportunity.'

'Not for me, miss.' I shake my head. 'What am I going to write about? Council estates and corner shops? I don't think so.'

Freya stands up quickly and for a moment I think I've annoyed her, but she walks over to her desk and slides open a drawer.

She takes out a DVD case and holds it up so I can see it. On the cover, there's a scruffy lad sneering at the camera and sticking two fingers up.

'Have you watched this film?'

I shake my head again. I don't think Mr Fox would be

too pleased if he knew Freya was encouraging students to watch this sort of thing.

'Why don't you watch it and tell me what you think when I see you on Friday?' Freya hands me the DVD. 'Then you can try to tell me again that working-class life isn't interesting.'

Reluctantly, I take it from her. It doesn't look like my sort of film at all.

I remember then I'm supposed to tell her I'm not coming to any more sessions, but instead I find myself nodding as I slide the DVD into my rucksack.

10

At break-time I meet up with the lads in the outer courtyard.

'So how did bowling go on Friday then, Cal?' Linford play-punches my arm.

'Yeah, good,' I say.

He glances at Jack but he doesn't say anything.

'Hey, guess who I saw going into that counsellor's office when I was over at the Admin block this morning?' Harry says.

For a second I think I'm actually going to throw up. Harry must have seen me sneaking into Freya's office.

Linford's eyes narrow. 'Who?'

I get ready to explain that I had to go but I won't be going again.

'Immi Grant.' Harry scowls. 'Walked in like he owned the place, he did, looked through me like I wasn't there while I waited for Miss Harris's photocopying. I reckon he's probably grassed you up for ruining his nosh in the dinner hall, Linford.'

I start to breathe normally.

'I knew it. They're trying to get me excluded through that flipping counsellor.' Linford clenches his jaw. 'They tried to see if you lot would grass me up and when that didn't work, they're trying it with that sponging Polack. Mr Fox is going to kick me out of this school for good, I know it.'

We all frown.

'And speaking of snitches . . .' Jack jabs his finger in the air.

Sergei Zurakowski walks by, looking at the floor.

'Hey Immi, I hear you've been blabbing to the school counsellor,' Linford yells after him. 'You dirty grass.'

I feel a thread of heat begin to climb my spine.

Sergei carries on walking and he doesn't look back.

'You'd better not drop me in it, you loser,' Linford growls, marching after him. When he catches up, he grabs Sergei's tatty rucksack and spins him roughly round with it.

'Please, stop this,' Sergei gasps, struggling to keep his balance.

'Only losers see the counsellor,' Linford snarls, pressing his face closer still. 'Sponging *foreign* losers, that's what my stepdad calls you lot.'

Sergei glances at me as he picks his rucksack up off the floor. He's going to tell him I had an appointment with Freya too.

'What you looking at Calum for?' Linford snaps. 'It's *me* you need to answer to.'

I take in a big gulp of air.

'Go on, say it, Immi: *I'm a loser*,' Linford demands.

Sergei says nothing.

'What did you go and see her for, then?' Linford grabs Sergei's blazer lapels. 'What did you tell her?'

'M-my tutor, he sent me there,' Sergei stammers, his eyes darting around the four of us. 'I did not ask to go, this is the truth.'

'So? They tried to send us too but none of us went there, snivelling like babies.' Linford tightens his grip on Sergei's blazer and pulls him in closer. 'Right, lads?'

'Right,' Jack agrees.

'Right,' Harry nods.

'Right,' I croak, forcing my fingernails into my palms.

Sergei looks at me and I feel heat pouring into my face and neck. My mouth is so dry I can't even say anything that might help to change the subject.

'But you . . .' Sergei starts to speak to me and then closes his mouth again.

'But what? What were you going to say?' Linford's eyes are dark and wild. He spits the words out, peppering Sergei's face with tiny flecks of saliva. 'Tell me, you sap.'

I close my eyes for a split-second and prepare for him to tell the others he saw me at Freya's office this morning.

'Nothing,' Sergei says quietly. 'I have nothing to say to you.'

'Yeah, well I have nothing to say to *you* either.' Linford snaps his knee up high and then stamps it down really hard, on to Sergei's foot.

Sergei lets out a howl and hops back on his good foot, his eyes watering.

Linford grabs his rucksack and tears open the top flap. He shakes it upside down until every single item in there lies scattered over the smooth pastel flagstones.

Snatches of laughter fill the air as a group of students gather to watch the show.

'Hey, what's this?' Linford snatches up a small photograph and hoots with glee. 'A flipping circus act?'

'Let's see.' Harry stands on his tiptoes and cranes his neck to see over Linford's shoulder.

'Please, give it back.' Sergei lunges for the photo but Linford holds it high above his head and crumples it into a loose ball before tossing it aside and walking away.

'See you, Immi.' Jack laughs, grinding the photograph under his shoe as he follows.

I look down at the creased image and see a smiling man wearing striped trousers, tucked into long black riding boots. There is a tall feather in his cap. He sits next to a pretty lady who is dressed in a long, floral skirt and wearing a bright, twisted headscarf on her head.

Sergei crouches down and picks up the photo like it's made of the finest silk. He presses it gently into the palm of his hand, trying in vain to flatten it again.

Anybody can see it's already ruined but he carries

on smoothing it anyway, as if the deep creases might magically disappear.

When I turn to walk away he realizes someone is still there and he looks up at me, dark eyes glistening under his overgrown fringe.

I meet his stare for just a second and his eyes seem to lock on to mine, making it impossible to turn away.

They are bottomless pools of misery and pain but I also see a flash of something raw and bright that refuses to be pushed aside.

I open my mouth to say thanks for not telling Linford about my appointment with Freya, but the words won't come.

I step over his empty rucksack and run to catch up with the others.

11

All through my afternoon lessons I feel a warm glow when I remember Dad will be home when I get back later, even though it's a Monday.

I can't remember the last time he was home on a weekday.

I'd like to watch the cricket together on telly but that woman is coming round later. What was her name? Angie. Still, I can't wait to meet her dog, I hope it's a Jack Russell or a Staffie. I could take him for a walk down by the canal if she'll let me, pretend he's mine for a bit. I bet Amelia and Spike would love him.

The lads are standing in a tight knot at the school gate. They stop talking and break apart as I walk over to them.

'Fancy a kickabout on the field later?' Jack asks me when I join them. 'We're meeting down there at six.'

'Nah, I can't.' For once, I'm telling the truth about my evening plans. 'We've got people coming round to the flat, later.'

'No worries.' Linford looks at Jack and Harry. 'We can manage without Cal.'

A tightness settles on my chest.

'See you tomorrow then, yeah?' I call as they walk off, but they can't have heard me because nobody answers.

As soon as I open the door, I hear voices in the flat. It's usually deathly quiet in here when I get home from school, so it feels strange, but nice.

I dump my rucksack on the kitchen floor and slip off my shoes before walking into the lounge. I see a pretty, slim woman with long pale hair sitting on our settee next to Dad. My heart begins to thump.

I glance around the room but there's no dog in here. Maybe she tied him up round the back so Dad can surprise me with him later.

Dad stands up and strides over to me. He's got his best jeans on and what looks like a brand-new T-shirt. And he's had a shave.

'This is our Calum.' Dad beams, guiding me over to her like I might run off. 'This is my lad.'

'I am so happy to meet you, Calum.' She's got a strong foreign accent I didn't expect, but speaks very good English. She holds out her hand. 'My name is Angelika; Angie to my friends.'

'Me and Angie met when I was on site doing some clearance work for a contractor at the university,' Dad explains. 'The wind took her umbrella off and I chased it down, brought it back for her.'

'My hero!' Angie giggles.

77

'When you put your head out of that classroom window and we started talking, well –' Dad's face flushes like a schoolboy – 'I thought all my Christmases had come at once.'

It's embarrassing, watching the two of them.

She's probably a cleaner at the university or something. According to Linford, his stepdad says they're all coming over in droves and taking the unskilled jobs from local people.

The room smells of flowers and talcum powder. She holds out her hand.

'Hello, Calum.'

'Hello.' I shuffle my feet.

There's a beat of silence, then Dad says, 'I'll make us all a drink.'

He disappears into the kitchen and I feel like running after him.

'Come. Sit here, Calum,' Angie says, patting the seat next to her.

My head feels like it is being boiled.

'So, Calum, what do you enjoy doing in your free time?'

I sit down and inspect my nails.

'Dunno really. Watching films and footie mainly.'

Angie laughs, a silvery tinkle that feels out of place in our quiet flat.

'OK, that is what you like watching. But what do you like *doing*?'

I'm distracted by the sound of the loo flushing across the hall. I can hear Dad pottering around in the kitchen, clinking cups. But if he's in the kitchen, who is . . .

A figure appears in the doorway. My mouth drops open and I jump up off the settee.

For a second I freeze, thinking he's wandered in here off the street to cause trouble. And then Dad's words come back to me: *she's bringing someone with her*. The heat drains out of my face.

'Calum, meet Sergei.' Angie smiles. 'He is my son.'

Sergei Zurakowski steps into the room. His face has turned the colour of the uncooked sausages on Mrs Brewster's barbecue. He probably looks even more shocked than I do, if that's even possible.

We stand staring at each other with open mouths.

Dad appears behind him holding a tray with four steaming mugs and a plate of custard creams.

'So, I see you two have met at last.' He beams, oblivious. He places the tray on the chipped pine sideboard.

Angie peers in turn at us both like she's watching a tennis match.

'Wait.' Angie's smile fades a touch. 'Do you boys know already each other?'

'From school,' I say with a nod, tapping my fingers on the sides of my thighs.

'Yes, we see each other quite a lot at school, don't we,

Calum?' Sergei looks over at me, narrowing his eyes. 'We were together briefly this afternoon, in fact. I ran into Calum and his friends.'

Very clever.

'That's brilliant! It's a small world.' Dad laughs. 'Tell you the truth, I was a bit nervous about you two lads getting on but it looks as though the four of us are going to be a match made in heaven – eh, Angie?'

'I do hope so,' she says softly, watching Sergei's face.

Dad grins and winks at me and I open my mouth to speak but nothing comes out.

All I can think is, *How the hell am I going to explain this to Linford?*

Dad announces that our 'guests' will be staying with us a while.

Me and Sergei both look up sharply.

'We thought we would surprise you,' Angie tells us.

'Makes no sense being stuck in a poky bed and breakfast when you can stay here with us.' He beams at Angie and she nods.

'Yeah, stay here in this poky flat that's barely big enough for the two of us,' I mutter.

'Calum, that's enough!' Dad snaps.

'I would rather stay in the bed and breakfast.' Sergei scowls at his mum. 'The university said the staff accommodation would be ready soon, so why can't we just wait? You did not say anything about staying *here*.'

'Pete only made his kind offer at the weekend, Sergei,' Angie replies. 'Neither of us like the bed and breakfast. It is much better here, yes?'

'No, Mama.' Sergei folds his arms in a huff. 'It is not better here, and anyway, what about all our stuff?'

'I packed everything up today while you were at school.' She beams. 'Pete already brought it across here to surprise you!'

'It is a surprise all right.' Sergei glowers. 'But not such a good one.'

Dad coughs.

'Cal, I've put the camp bed and a quilt in your bedroom for Sergei.' Dad's keeping his voice jolly but his eyes are flashing me an unspoken warning to be nice. 'Why don't you two lads go and put it up together now, get to know each other a bit better? I'm sure you'll soon be best mates.'

Sergei snorts.

I glare at Dad but he isn't even looking at me. I walk out of the room across the tiny hallway and Sergei follows. Once we're in my bedroom, I close the door.

'What the hell are you doing?' I round on him. 'Why are you even here?'

'Do you think I want to be here, with *you*?' Sergei takes a step towards me, his face thunderous.

'Yeah, well you're the one who's come here. If

81

you don't like it, you can—'

'Do you think this is my choice, to be here with *you* when you hate me so much?' He raises his voice and I glance at the door, hoping Dad and Angie aren't listening outside. 'How was I supposed to know that Mama's new boyfriend was the father of the school bully?'

'I don't believe this.' I groan, sinking down on to my bed and holding my head in my hands. 'This is seriously my worst nightmare.'

Sergei releases a bitter laugh. 'Believe me, it is my worst nightmare also.'

I snap my head up.

'Yeah, I bet it is. But this is *my* home and *my* dad we're talking about. You don't even belong here.'

He moves towards me, his fists balled and his body tense like he's going to spring for me. He looks different here in my room to how he looks at school. Taller, broader. I stand up but I've no room to move with the bed behind me.

He stops suddenly and his shoulders sag. 'What is the use? You cannot reason with ignorance.'

'Who are you calling ignorant?' I take my chance and step away from the bed. If he wants to start on me then he can have a go and get what's coming. This is my home, not his.

Sergei pushes the camp bed flat and starts to unfold it. '*I do not belong here*. This is what you tell me every day at school and now you tell it to me here, in your home. I understand now, OK, Calum? Perhaps you can tell your friends I have the message now, so they stop doing *this* –' He smacks his fist into his open hand.

I think about how Angie looked at him when she realized we knew each other.

'Are you going to tell them?' I nod towards the lounge. 'About the stuff that happens at school?'

Sergei doesn't answer but he doesn't look away, either.

He pulls out the bed's metal legs and stands back.

'Do what you like anyway.' I shrug. 'It's not me that gives you a hard time.'

'But you are there when this hard time happens, yes?'

'Yeah, but I don't actually *do* anything to you. Linford, yes, sometimes Jack or Harry, but not me.'

'You watch them do it. You laugh in all the right places, Calum.'

I stand up and walk over to the window. I have to shuffle sideways because his camp bed has taken up all the floor space.

The grass out back is so long the little path down to the gate has nearly disappeared.

'Why can't you just stay out of their way?' I turn round when he doesn't answer. 'You didn't have to walk by us today, did you? You could've gone the long way round.'

Sergei shakes his head slowly. He presses his lips

together like he is trying hard to keep in lots of things he'd quite like to say.

He shakes out the fusty-smelling quilt that has been stuck in the back of the airing cupboard. He lays it carefully on top of the bed before walking over to the door.

'You can ignore me all you like.' I fold my arms. 'Fact is, *I don't do anything.*'

'Exactly, Calum.' He reaches for the handle and then turns around and looks right at me. 'While your friends make so many people's lives at school a misery, you do nothing. What a hero you are.'

Then he walks out and closes the bedroom door behind him.

We eat pizza then carrot cake while we watch catch-up *You've Been Framed* on TV, but I can't taste any of the food and each mouthful feels dry and hard, like I'm swallowing marbles.

I sit at one side of the room and Sergei sits at the other. Dad and Angie are glued together on the couch, and when Dad pours their third glass of wine, she hooks her leg over his knee and he puts his arm around her and twists a piece of her hair around his fingers.

I look away and take a swig of my pop.

Sergei will probably call Dad names later, even though his mum is being just as gross.

I keep staring stonily at the television screen. Someone has filmed an idiot swinging on a stringy rope over a stream and, predictably, he falls in.

Out of the corner of my eye I notice Angie whisper something to Dad.

'You two get off to your room if you like now, Cal,' Dad says as if he's doing us a favour. 'I know you'll want to watch one of your DVDs or get online, not sit with us old fuddy-duddies.'

Angie giggles and keeps repeating *fuddy-duddies*

as if it's the best joke ever.

Sergei shoots Dad a dark look, gets up and leaves the room.

I hear him slam his plate down in the kitchen and then my bedroom door opens, which makes want to scream at him to get out. He should be asking me if he can go in there, not acting as if this is *his* home now.

I don't want to go to my room while he's in there but I don't want to watch Dad and Angie getting cosy on the settee either, so I stand up and follow him.

'Close the door behind you, young 'un,' Dad calls and Angie giggles again.

I stand just outside my bedroom door and spy in through the gap.

Sergei sits very still on his thin, lumpy mattress looking down at a small open suitcase. As far as I can tell, it's full of scruffy old cardboard, the colour of worn-out rope.

After a minute or two I start to wonder why I'm standing out in the hallway like a loser while he's got my bedroom all to himself.

I push the door open with my foot and step inside. He doesn't look up.

'What's that?' I demand, pointing at the open case. 'There's no room in here for all your crap.'

'For your information, these are my buildings.'

'They don't look like buildings.' I take a few steps closer, peering down at the black lines and folds in the flat, thick paper. 'Just looks like a load of old cardboard to me.'

'It seems that you do not know everything there is to know, after all.' He smirks at me and I feel like upending his stupid suitcase on the floor.

'You'll have to keep all that stuff over your side. My bedroom's too cramped as it is.' I climb over his stuff and sit on my own bed. 'When are you and your mum getting your own place?'

'I do not know,' he says. There are a few moments' silence before he speaks again. 'The sooner it happens then the better we will all feel, yes?'

'Too right,' I mumble, plumping my pillows up behind me. 'Can't come soon enough for me.'

'You have some good film pictures here,' he says, nodding to the posters that cover my walls. 'I have seen all the *Die Hard* movies.'

'Good for you.'

'I have never seen so many films.' He's staring at the neat columns of DVDs piled up at the end of my bed, against the wall.

I don't answer him.

He points to the scuffed shelf his side of the wall. 'Is there room on here for some of my things?'

The shelf is mostly empty, just a few old books and

magazines on there that I haven't looked at for ages. I think about saying no just to be mean but I can't be bothered. I just want him to go away or shut up. Preferably both.

'Suppose so.' I sigh. 'If it keeps your stuff out of my way.'

'Thank you, you are very kind,' he says, but he doesn't sound as though he means it at all.

I watch as he touches the pile of crappy old cardboard again like it's something precious instead of the load of garbage it actually is.

On top of taking up half my bedroom, Sergei Zurakowski also talks in his sleep. All flipping night. Gobbledegook that sounds like 'jar-deck and bark-char'. He repeats it over and over again and only stops when I throw my pillow at him.

It goes without saying I hardly sleep a wink.

Then, when I'm finally fast asleep and on a film set in Hollywood talking to Vin Diesel, he wakes me up.

'Good morning.'

I open one eye to see him sitting up in bed, watching me. I grunt and pull the quilt over my head.

'It is seven o'clock, Calum, time to rise.'

I snatch the quilt down and glare at him.

'Seven o'clock? I don't get up until eight.' The quilt goes over my head again.

'But we have to shower and have breakfast. We have to tidy up this room, yes?'

'Get lost,' I growl.

I hear him sigh and start to move around.

He pads out of the bedroom and the loo flushes. I try to get back to my dream, the bit where the director asks me to act as a stand-in for Vin Diesel, but it's all dissolved now. Gone.

He comes back into the room and closes the door. Then the banging, thumping, sighing starts.

I snatch the quilt off my head again.

'Can't you just be quiet? What the hell are you doing?'

'I am unpacking my things,' he says. He's opened the bigger suitcase under the window now, taking up the last small square of space there was to stand there.

'I don't know why you're bothering taking all that stuff out. With any luck, you won't be staying here that long.'

But he just laughs and carries on unpacking as if I haven't said a word.

I'm tying my shoelaces in the hallway when Sergei appears.

'Ready?'

I look up at him. 'Ready for what?'

'To walk to school, of course.' He hoists his rucksack higher on to his back.

89

'Are you crazy? I'm not walking in with you.' Linford's face floats into my mind. 'I don't care when or how you get to school but you're not walking in with me.'

I grab my own rucksack and push by him.

As I pass Dad's bedroom, the door opens and Angie appears.

'You two boys have a good day, yes?' She yawns and rubs her eyes. She's tied her hair back and her pink lipstick is gone.

Dad appears in his boxer shorts behind her, his hair stuck up into salt-and-pepper tufts.

'Good to see you lads getting on,' he says, clueless as usual. 'I'm home again tonight, Cal, so see you then.'

I suddenly realize that when Dad goes away on a job again, I'll be alone with Sergei and his mum.

I'll be outnumbered in my own home.

13

After saying goodbye to Dad and Angie, me and Sergei leave the flat together.

As soon as we get out on to the street, I stride off on my own and keep on walking at a good speed. As I turn off the estate to head up the hill, I take a sly look over my shoulder. Sergei is still behind me and looks as though he is purposely hanging back. He stops outside the community centre and studies something pinned to the fence. The next time I turn around I can't see him at all.

I arrive at school a bit early, with walking so fast. I hang around the gates a while but the lads don't appear in our usual meeting spot. I eventually find them in the inner courtyard.

Harry is saying something to the others but he stops talking when I get closer.

'I wondered where you lot were.' I sidle up to them.

Linford looks up at me and then looks back down at his phone.

'How was football last night?' I say after a bit.

At first I don't think anyone is going to answer, then Jack speaks.

'It was good.'

My skin is crawling, like there's something nasty creeping up on me that I can't see.

'How was your evening?' Linford says with a smirk. 'Enjoy spending it with your visitors, did you?'

'It was OK,' I say, feeling sick when I think who it was.

'Can you smell summat?' Harry says, looking round. 'There's a rotten smell around here somewhere.'

Jack laughs and I think for a moment Harry means me, and then I look round and see Sergei walking across the courtyard. Despite me telling him to keep out of Linford's way at school, here he is, asking for trouble again.

'Yo, Immi,' Linford calls. 'When you pissing off back home, then?'

For a second I think Sergei is heading over to us. My heart hammers, making it difficult to calm my thoughts down and think.

What am I going to say if he tells Linford he's staying at our flat? Is it best to deny it or admit it? There is no way Linford will believe I knew nothing about Sergei staying with us until last night.

But Sergei stays silent and walks straight by us. I close my eyes and say a silent thanks.

Linford spits his chewing gum out like a bullet and it hits Sergei on the arm. He carries on walking, eyes focused straight ahead.

'What's his problem?' Linford looks at him and back

at me. 'He needs teaching a proper lesson in manners, right, Cal?'

Sergei glances over and locks eyes with me.

'Just ignore him,' I say, looking down at my feet. 'He's not worth the effort.'

When I look up again, Linford is staring at me through narrowed eyes.

After school I spot the lads walking away from the gates. I break into a jog and catch up with them.

'What's happening?' I say.

'We're going to that new chippy that's opened up on Mapperley Top,' Harry replies.

'I'll come with you.' I fall in line just in time to catch a look that passes between Linford and Jack. 'That's OK, isn't it?' I bite my inside cheek as I wait for Linford to answer.

He shrugs. 'If you like.'

I don't know why things feel so strained. I'm relieved when, after a few minutes, we're chatting about the football results and how Man U are doing in the league. Everything seems to be back to normal and I begin to wonder if I'm imagining this new awkwardness that appears to sit between me and them.

At the chippy I pretend I'm not hungry. I haven't got enough coins in my pocket to buy even a small bag of chips.

Linford and Jack both get trays stacked with meat pie, chips and gravy and sit on the low wall outside the shop. I wait inside with Harry and watch as the server ladles curry sauce over an enormous tray of chips. My mouth waters.

Harry grabs two plastic forks and hands me one.

'You'll have to help me out here, Cal; there's loads more than I thought.'

Our eyes meet for just a second. I think he knows why I haven't ordered anything.

'Thanks, mate,' I mutter.

We sit down on the wall and everybody is quiet for a few minutes, shovelling the delicious hot food in.

We hear the booming bass beat first and then watch as a silver Mercedes cruises slowly past, the tinted windows rolled down but not far enough to see who is inside.

The car stops in front of us and the front passenger-side window glides all the way down.

'Enjoying your tea, ladies?' a voice shouts above the beat.

I see a mouth with a gold tooth first, then a thin, spotty face appears.

Linford laughs, puts his tray down on the wall and walks over to the car. He touches fists with the passenger.

'You boys are growing up fast.' The man grins, turning to whoever is driving. 'You come see us when you ready to rumble, yeah? We pay well if you want to do some stuff for us.'

I can guess the sort of stuff he means.

He looks at us all in turn.

'Say what?' He cups his hand to his ear.

'Yeah,' we all chant in unison.

I don't know what they do for a living but I've got a pretty good idea. Rumour is, most of them have done time inside, and from what I can see, they drive around the estates all day long, meeting up with people and pocketing money after long handshakes.

'Stay clear of that shower of no-hopers,' Dad told me when I started at the Comp. 'They're bad news. All of them.'

I lean forward, trying to see who is driving the car, but the tinted window is moving up again and I'm not fast enough.

The car moves off and Linford puts his hand up, watching them go before sitting down with his food again. He lets out a sigh of what sounds like relief.

I watch him as he puts a couple of chips in his mouth and chews slowly, scanning the road ahead, as if he wants to make sure the car has definitely gone.

If I didn't know him better, I'd say his bravado seems to have deserted him. He's gone all pale and quiet.

We sit on the wall for ages after we've finished eating. I'm glad. Even though nobody is saying much,

I don't feel like going home yet.

I glance sideways at Linford. He's staring at the floor, digging sharply at the pebbles and chips of asphalt with his shoe, as if they're to blame for something.

We've known each other since primary school but I don't know where all the laughter went between us. It's like it just seeped away down into the gutter.

Harry and Jack live on the opposite side of the estate, so they set off walking home together.

'Fancy walking back the long way?' I say to Linford. If we walk around the edge of the estate, we pass both our streets.

'Nah, I've got to call at the shop,' he says, standing up. 'See ya.'

I sit on the wall on my own for a bit. The new chippy gets busy with everybody calling in after work for their tea. Sharing Harry's food has made me hungrier, if anything. I wonder if there is anything in to eat at home and then I think about Sergei and his mum being there and my appetite fades a bit.

I stand up and out of nowhere I get this idea that if I run, I might be able to catch Linford up before he gets home. I could talk to him without the others listening – maybe it's a chance to set things straight between us again.

Something has changed in our friendship but I don't know what. It feels like standing onstage and glancing behind you to find someone changed the set without saying anything and you don't know the part you're supposed to be playing any more.

If I can talk to Linford now, just the two of us, maybe we can clear the air.

But when I look in the direction he walked off, he's nowhere to be seen. He must have rushed home. By the time I get to Linford's street I'm puffing like an old man. I stop running and turn the corner and there he is, just about to walk in his front gate.

'Linford!'

He turns round and when he sees it's me, his face falls. He pushes at the gate. The bottom hinge is broken and it scrapes on the concrete path, making a sharp sound like a dry cough.

'What's up?' he barks, taking a step away from the gate.

'I just wanted to talk to you. I –'

Linford's head whips round as his front door flies open.

A burly man with a firm round belly and ruddy cheeks fills the doorway.

'What time d'ya call this? You were supposed to be back before six to look after your sister, you little runt.' He steps out of the door and stomps towards the gate in socked feet, swigging from a can of lager. 'Where the hell have you been?'

It's ages since I've seen Linford's stepdad and he looks

almost unrecognizable. He's put on loads of weight and his head looks over-inflated, like a red balloon stuck on his meaty shoulders.

'S-sorry, Dad, I forgot,' Linford stammers, his face draining of colour. 'We went for some tea.'

Linford glances back at me and I give an eager nod to back him up. He twists and pulls at his fingers, as if he's trying to remove a pair of invisible gloves.

'If I get that frigging school on my back again you're dead, d'ya hear me? Last time that Head Teacher of yours reckoned I could get fined and if I do, I'm going to—'

'I'm not in any trouble, Dad.' Linford shoots me a warning look.

I know he's embarrassed and wants me to go, but I can't move.

'Who said you can speak, eh?' His dad presses his florid face closer, just like I've seen Linford do with others at school.

Linford doesn't cheek back, he doesn't puff his chest out and pull himself up to his full height. Instead, he winces and half closes his eyes. His lips press into a thin, tight line like he is steeling himself for something.

My mouth hangs open. Linford's swagger has melted into thin air.

'I—' Before he can finish his sentence, Linford's stepdad grabs him by the scruff of his neck and stares down into his eyes.

I wait for Linford to push back and pull free. I wait for his fists to clench so tight his knuckles turn white like when he's mad at school. But that doesn't happen.

The Linford I know has disappeared and left a shrunken, pale boy in his place.

'Get in the house,' his stepdad growls. 'Now.'

I want to say something to get Linford out of trouble. I want to run away, back to our flat. Even if Sergei and his mum are there, I don't care. At least I feel safe at home.

Instead, I stand rooted to the spot, watching as Linford follows his stepdad meekly back indoors like a lost lamb.

He turns at the last moment and looks at me and I get a glimpse of the boy I've been friends with since primary school.

★

EXT. ST ANN'S PRIMARY SCHOOL PLAYGROUND –
DAY
Two BOYS kicking a football to each other
across the yard.

BOY ONE
I'm gonna play for Manchester United when
I'm older.

BOY TWO
(runs after ball half-heartedly)
That's just a stupid dream.

99

BOY ONE

You always used to say you were gonna play
for them, too.

BOY TWO places foot on ball to stop it
rolling. He leans back against brick wall
and closes his eyes.

BOY ONE

What's up, mate?

BOY TWO

Mum's getting married to Martin. She told me
last night.

BOY ONE

You like Martin, don't you?

BOY TWO

(*hesitantly*)

Yeah, but Mum says I've got to call him
'Dad'.

BOY ONE

But he's not your dad.

BOY TWO
(*sighs*)

I know. But Mum says my real dad is as good
as dead and that Martin is my new dad now.

He ignores the ball and leans back on the
wall, looking downcast.

BOY ONE
Who *is* your real dad?

BOY TWO
(*quietly, eyes glistening*)
I don't know. I never met him.

END SCENE.

14

When I get back, the flat is empty.

In the fridge, I find a big plate of triangular-cut sandwiches covered over with cling film. I stuff one into my mouth and put another couple on a plate. In the cupboard, there's a multi-bag of assorted crisps, and I choose a pack of cheese and onion. I feel like a kid at Christmas. I pour a glass of juice and take the food straight to my bedroom. After wolfing it down, I lie on my bed in the gloom for a bit. I don't want sunshine and summer; it feels out of place after what just happened outside Linford's place.

I remember a couple of years ago, Linford's stepdad got a bonus at work and took all four of us to the go-kart track in Colwick. He paid for everything and we all went for burgers afterwards, too.

We all had so much fun that day, we never stopped laughing.

It was only a few months later Linford mentioned in passing that his stepdad had lost his job. That's the last I'd heard of him until today, but judging by what I've seen today, Linford has been going home to him each night and dealing with his moods.

I close my eyes and inhale, letting the breath out slowly. Usually when I get home I put the telly straight on, but for once I don't mind the quiet. I've never bothered spending that much time in my bedroom, with Dad being away a lot. I thought of it just as somewhere to sleep.

Now Sergei's here, I've got no place where I can just be me – not even in my own room. Every time I want to move around, I have to climb over all his stuff. I keep walking backwards and forwards on purpose so I trip over it all and have a reason to feel so angry. He's folded his clothes in two neat piles next to a small pyramid of socks and undies. I kick out at one of the piles.

It makes my guts burn and that feels better than feeling there's nothing I can do about the situation.

I squeeze my eyes shut and sniff. There's a different smell in the air since he came. Not unpleasant or anything, just different – but I don't like it. Funny, I never realized me and Dad had our own smell until a new one came along. I reckon I could spot Dad at a distance just by the smell of brick dust and cement that invades the house when he gets home from a building-site job.

After a bit, I get up off the bed and snap on the light. I curse when I trip over something on the floor – it's the pile of books and magazines that Sergei has dumped off the shelf I let him use.

I turn round to look and see a model of the Empire

State Building sitting proudly on the shelf. *In my bedroom.* It's not that big really, but somehow it fills the room. It looks sort of majestic, like it has a presence all on its own.

I walk over and run my fingers over the lettering at the bottom of the model. The detailing is impressive. The windows seem as if they stand proud of the building but feel smooth under my fingertips. It doesn't look like a bit of old folded cardboard with black lines scrawled all over it any more.

I can almost imagine people in there, buzzing around at the ticket turnstiles. Tourists and students, eager to climb to the top to see the view of New York City. Mums and dads and their kids, or maybe couples and folks on their own. People celebrating birthdays and special occasions, all wanting that elusive snap taken right at the top for their Facebook profile, or just to show family and friends back home.

The photo that will say, *I was there. I went to the Empire State Building and saw New York City. I did it.*

I wish I had that photo. I wonder briefly if I'll ever go there, but I don't know one person round here who's been and it just seems like another daft dream.

'Two hundred and thirty-four floors.' Sergei's voice floats into the room from the doorway. 'The Empire State Building was built in 1930.'

How come he knows so much about everything,

coming from a poky little town in Poland? I turn away from the model and pick up my notebook and pen. I've started to jot down a few ideas for my screenplay but nothing's coming together yet.

'It is built to scale, an exact replica of the real thing,' he says, shuffling around his bed to get to it.

He places his fingers delicately at the front edges of the building and bends his knees. His eyes scan across its width, checking everything is still level.

'I didn't move it if that's what you're worried about.' I slouch back on to my bed.

'I'm not worried about it at all,' he says. 'Glad you like it, though.'

I didn't even say I liked it. I leaf blindly through my notebook, wishing he'd go and sit in the living room or something and take his stupid model with him.

'Do you like it, Calum?'

''S'all right.' I shrug. 'If you're into that kind of thing.'

He sits at the end of my bed. I stretch out my legs until my feet push against him.

'If you would like, I can show you how I assembled the building.'

I don't answer him. He just can't take a hint.

'We share a room now, Calum. We could try to become friends,' he says with a sigh. 'Maybe I'll even forgive you for being such an idiot at school. What do you say?'

'I say why don't you sit on your *own* bed, for starters.'

105

I snap the notebook closed and glare at him. Who the hell does he think he is? Muscling his way into my life, my home, my bedroom. 'Why don't you find something to do?'

He rolls his eyes and clambers back over to his squeaky camp bed.

'We could just talk for a while if you prefer,' he drones on. 'Maybe you would like to tell me why you think only you and your friends are entitled to be happy at school?'

Happy! He's even more stupid than he looks.

'If you're not going to move then I will.' I slide off my bed and push my way past him. 'Just stay out of my way.'

I slam the door on my way out.

Later, when Sergei and Angie are watching TV, I corner Dad in the kitchen.

'How long are they staying here for?' I hiss.

'Don't you like them?' His face falls. 'You seem to be getting on really well with Sergei.'

'You should have told me they were coming.' I bite my lip. 'It's a shock them just turning up like this.'

'I'm sorry, lad.' Dad puts down the tea caddy and lays his hand on my shoulder. 'I've not handled it very well, have I? But I never expected to meet anyone or thought things would move this quickly. But you know, sometimes life throws you an opportunity that you just can't pass on.'

'But you hardly know Angie, Dad.' I don't want to make him feel bad but this is stuff that needs saying. 'I mean, you haven't had *time* to properly get to know her, have you?'

'I know what you're saying, son. And I know this is going to sound crazy. But when you get to my age, you get to be a pretty good judge of character, and we've spent a lot of time talking and getting to know each other since we first met that day at the university.'

He's right, it does sound crazy.

'It suited all our circumstances to ask them if they wanted to move in here rather than be stuck in some crabby B-and-B. Sharing the bills is a big relief for both me and Angie. And I thought you'd like having a lad your own age around.'

'You thought I'd like giving up half my bedroom to a complete stranger? Sergei's got a bad attitude, you just don't see it.'

I don't want to hurt Dad but my head feels full of building pressure.

Dad runs a hand through his hair.

'I thought it'd be a bit of company for you,' he mumbles. 'When I'm away, I mean. And it turns out you knew each other from school, so Sergei's hardly a complete stranger, is he?'

Now my head feels like it's going to explode.

'You can't just bring other people in to take your place,' I snap. *'You're* the one who should be here, at home. Not them.'

Dad's eyes widen at my outburst just as the door opens and Angie walks in.

'So, what are you two boys up to in here?' She grins, catching Dad round his waist and nuzzling her face into his chest. *Ugh.*

'We were just saying how nice it is having you two around,' Dad simpers. 'Right, Calum?'

I can't say anything without the truth spilling out so I reach up to the cupboard and take out the biscuit barrel.

'I know adjusting can be difficult, Calum.' She walks over and touches my arm lightly. 'Change is never easy. Sergei and I, we have had very big changes in our lives also.'

I should just walk away but instead I freeze, with my fingers stuck down among the custard creams.

'We miss home,' she says faintly, and her eyes fade far away.

'Why don't you go back there, then?' The words slip out before I can bite them back.

'Calum!' Dad throws me a warning look.

'I'm not being rude,' I say, but I am really. I don't care.

Like Linford says, *they're* the ones who've come over to this country. Nobody forced them, right? Angie might

108

have even planned all along on meeting someone gullible like Dad.

I look away from Dad's frown and feel the dry biscuit crumbs rubbing and chafing as I wriggle my fingers.

'I only meant that if you miss home that much, you could always go back,' I say.

Angie smiles and shakes her head at Dad to silence him.

'It's a fair question, Pete.' She looks back at me. 'Things were very difficult for Sergei and me back in Poland, Calum. In fact, the situation got very dangerous. When Nottingham Trent University offered me the teaching placement, it was the perfect chance for us to make a fresh start.'

Teaching placement? I'd assumed she'd latched on to Dad because she had a low-paid cleaning job. I pull my hand out of the biscuit tin and dust off the crumbs.

'Moving in here so quickly has been a shock for all of us, I think.'

Dad never said they were *moving in*. Only yesterday, he said they'd just be staying a few nights. 'I thought you said the university was sorting you out with accommodation?' I remarked. If she really was a teacher, surely they'd be happy to sort a place out for her, coming over from a foreign country?

'Yes, they did say that in my Skype interview,' Angie tells me. 'But the staff quarters have fallen behind in the refurbishment schedule and so we must wait longer than expected.'

Very convenient.

'Don't you have any other family here?' I ask, and her eyes dart over to Sergei's. He looks at his feet.

'No. No, we don't,' Angie says quickly.

Something isn't adding up here. Something isn't right. But I can't put my finger on what, apart from the fact they seem to both be acting shiftily.

I glance at Dad and see he is frowning, so I don't say anything else.

I don't feel like joining them in the living room and playing happy families, so I go to my room and lie on the bed staring at the ceiling.

The white paint has thinned in places, and patches of the old dirty cream colour are showing through. Like most things in this flat, it needs refreshing, updating.

I wonder if Linford is in his bedroom too, keeping out of his stepdad's way. I wouldn't want any of the lads to see my tip of a room even if Sergei wasn't here.

I glance over at the *Toy Story 3* lampshade I grew out of about four or five years ago. I can remember Dad taking me to the cinema at the Cornerhouse to see the film and then we had a burger afterwards.

He didn't work away as much in those days.

He's too busy now to worry about things like replacing lampshades and repainting – apart from his own bedroom of course. He's always too busy to go to the cinema, although now Angie and Sergei are here, he seems to want to be around an awful lot more.

I don't know why I'm thinking about stuff that doesn't matter. I've got ninety-nine problems and my lampshade isn't one of them. But there *is* one big problem in particular that needs sorting out pronto.

I need to work out how I'm going to break the bad news to the lads. How am I going to tell them that Sergei and his mum have just moved into our flat, without looking like I've known about it all along?

It feels as if I've kept it from them on purpose but I really hadn't got a clue who Dad had in mind when he said we had visitors coming round. Perhaps if I could explain everything from the very beginning, Linford would be able to see that I haven't had a say in it. He should know all about putting up with crap from your parents. I could explain how, after all these years, Dad randomly announced he'd met someone and how I thought she was bringing a dog but the dog actually turned out to be Sergei Zurakowski.

I suppose even *I* wouldn't believe that, even if it is the truth.

I barely get five minutes' peace before the bedroom door opens and Sergei's dour face appears.

'What are you up to in here, Calum?'

'Who wants to know?'

Sergei's mouth hovers on the edge of a grin like he's trying to decide if I'm joking with him.

'I am asking because I am wondering why you choose to be in here, all alone,' he says.

'Well, last time I looked, this was *my* bedroom.' I focus on a cobweb on the ceiling. 'I don't need an excuse to spend time in here and I don't have to explain myself to you.'

'I came to see if you wanted to watch TV with us in the *salon*?'

'Salon? I don't need my hair cut, thanks.'

'I mean the living room, as your father calls it. *Salon*, it is a Polish term for the room in which all the family sits together.'

'Yeah, well you're not in Poland now, are you?' I snatch up a magazine. 'More's the pity.'

'Why have you such hatred in your heart?'

'I don't know what you're talking about.'

'You and your friends, you hate anyone who is different. That is the truth.'

'Why don't you just go and watch TV?' I pretend to read the magazine. 'I don't want to hear your lecture, thanks.'

'I am trying to understand.' He frowns. 'Understand what makes you behave the way you do.'

'Save it,' I huff. 'When Brexit gets going, it won't make any difference cos you'll be gone anyway.'

He sits on his bed facing me.

'Stop staring at me.' I stare back at him.

'It is a free country.' He smiles. 'I can look where I like. I do not need your permission.'

I kick my foot forward and purposely miss him. He doesn't flinch.

'Not so brave at school, are you?' I taunt him.

'Neither are you.' He kicks back and misses me only because I scoot to the left. 'Not so brave when your friends are not around.'

I feel like kicking him, and this time making sure I don't miss. But there's something in his eyes that stops me. Something dangerous and daring . . . a side I haven't seen at school.

'I want you out of my room,' I say.

'I cannot do that because I have more buildings I must assemble,' he says, as if making up stupid cardboard models is a proper job he gets paid to do.

'*More* buildings?' I glare at him. 'Where do you think you're going to put them? You've already filled my room to bursting with your tat.'

'I will build only my favourites,' he continues, undeterred. 'They should fit easily on my shelf.'

Did he just say *his* shelf?

I just don't see the point in spending time making stupid toy buildings. He's obviously had his mum running round after him in Poland while he sits and puts together cardboard models like a big kid instead of having to worry if there's enough electricity on the meter card or food to manage through until the end of the week. Welcome to my world.

'You see, the bases are quite small and take up very little room because it is the height that needs most of the space.'

'Yeah, I'm guessing that's why they call them skyscrapers,' I say, rolling my eyes.

Sergei doesn't reply; he stands up and walks over to the Empire State Building.

'The height is not the most important thing in the building process.' He traces a finger up from the base to the pointed tip of the model.

'But it's the best thing,' I remark. 'The height is the whole point of building skyscrapers, to create an impressive city skyline.'

I think about the picture I have on my phone of The Shard with its mirrored angles that slice up the sky. So beautiful and impossibly high.

In the spring term there had been a Year Eight school trip organized to London. Dad signed the consent form but forgot to leave the money and he was working away all week.

Mrs Barnes said if I brought my money the next day I could keep my place, but in the end I pretended I wasn't bothered about going. I could hardly tell her I was home alone all week and wouldn't see Dad again until Saturday.

'Yes, Calum, but its height is the most *fragile* thing and many situations could bring it down. Such as tremors, wind even.' Sergei taps the floor with his foot. 'The most impressive thing is what you cannot see.'

'The foundations.' I yawn, wishing he'd just go away. No such luck.

'Correct. The foundations of the actual building extend to fifty-five feet down from base. Impressive, yes?'

I ignore him but, as usual, it makes no difference.

'Without a solid base any structure is weak, no matter how strong or impressive it appears to be.'

I think about my idea for the screenplay competition. The theme is 'A Place I Want to Go' and I wonder . . . if that place could be a building that can take you up to the sky. Is the sky a place you can go?

I've never been anywhere really high, up away from this flat, this estate and the stuff that's happening at school. I could just start to write for my own entertainment, I don't even have to hand it in and get ridiculed.

It's weak at the moment, but maybe, just maybe, if I put some thought into planning it, the foundations of the story will grow stronger. For now, I'll keep it to myself.

Sergei is still rattling on. I can't believe I'm sitting here listening to him. As if *he* knows anything.

I get up off the bed and walk out of the room. All

thoughts of silly competitions are gone, suddenly pushed away by a real concern.

I still don't know how I'm going to explain everything to Linford.

15

'I'm just popping out,' I call, and shut the door before Dad can ask me to get him anything from the shop.

I just need to stretch my legs and get some fresh air. I feel like I can't move in that flat, with Sergei and his mum there, everywhere I look.

I head down towards the canal.

There are crowds of girls outside the Motorpoint Arena. They are clustered around their mobile phones, sharing pictures, speaking excitedly in low voices, and I wonder what boy band is playing tonight.

I walk past the BBC Radio Nottingham building on London Road. There's probably someone famous in there waiting to be interviewed by the presenters, telling the listeners all about their fabulous life.

I'm nearing the entrance to the canal bank now.

Cars stream by me on the busy road leading to Trent Bridge, past the train station and tower-block hotels. Apartment buildings and offices line up like concrete soldiers on the edge of the pavement, and I try not to breathe in too deeply, as the air is thick with exhaust fumes.

On this side of the road is the water, the cyclists,

the joggers. There are ducks and I even spot a couple of swans, serenely gliding away from me.

I take a sharp left and descend the steep steps to the canal side. The hum of the traffic fades down here and as I walk, watching the oily black swell of the water, my jumbled thoughts start to fade a little.

Another five minutes of walking at a good pace and *My Fair Lady* comes into view. The glossy primary colours I first thought of as gaudy brighten my mood now as I approach. A thin coil of smoke winds up from the wood-burner chimney at the back, and the pots of geraniums and leafy plants quiver slightly in the breeze as if they sense my presence.

I was hoping someone might be out on deck but there is no sign of life; the boat looks all locked up. I walk alongside it and bend down to peer through the window. It's difficult to see inside, through the lace and the curtains.

Then suddenly Spike's beaming face appears from inside. He bangs on the glass and waves. Seconds later, the two small wooden doors at the end fly open and Amelia jumps up on to the deck.

'Calum! Come inside.'

I start to say I haven't really got time and I was only walking past, but the boat looks cosy through the open doors and Amelia will be disappointed. Plus, I don't want to go back to the flat yet. So I climb aboard.

Sandy is standing in the galley area.

'You arrived at the perfect time, Calum.' She smiles. 'I'm making hot chocolate, fancy a cup?'

'Sounds lovely, thanks,' I say.

'Come and sit down, Calum,' Amelia says, and we edge past Sandy and move to the end of the boat to sit near the warmth.

Spike stops bouncing around on the cushions and sits down next to me.

'Look, Calum, I drew Spiderman.'

He shows me his sketchpad. He's drawn Spiderman in pencil and it's not bad at all.

'That's brilliant, Spike,' I say. 'Wish I could draw.'

'What are your hobbies?' he asks.

'Dunno. Writing,' I say, surprising myself when I realize I mean it. 'I'm writing a screenplay that I might enter for a competition.'

I'm stretching the truth a bit because I haven't *actually* started writing. But all films start as an idea and I'm mulling one over in my head.

'Ooh, get you!' Amelia teases.

'I dunno though,' I add quickly. 'I haven't decided yet. I don't know if my idea is going to be good enough.'

'You should go for it.' Amelia nudges me. 'You can thank me when you're famous.'

'Yeah, right.' I snigger.

Spike looks up at me and his face breaks into a wide grin.

119

'I know! I can teach you to draw, if you like? My dad was a good drawer.'

'Great,' I say. 'I'd like that.'

Amelia looks at me over Spike's head and smiles. Not one of her mischievous grins this time; if anything she looks a bit sad. I wonder where her dad is but I don't ask.

I look around, watching Spike flicking through his sketchpad, Amelia warming her toes in front of the burner, and further up the boat Sandy whisking a jug of hot chocolate up into an impressive froth.

I only just met these people but I feel welcome and relaxed, like I'm one of the family. So much better than being stuck in the flat with those two interlopers.

Sandy brings our drinks over and we sit together in companionable silence for a few minutes.

'How come you're down by the canal at this time?' Amelia says after a while. There's a faint rim of creamy chocolate milk around her mouth. 'It's nearly eight o'clock. I've never seen you around here in the evening.'

I shrug. 'Just fancied getting out of the flat.'

'Why?' Spike asks. 'Don't you like your flat?'

'Not really,' I say honestly. 'It's tiny and it's stuck in the middle of a housing estate.'

'*My Fair Lady* is tiny,' Spike remarks. 'But we still love living on her, don't we, Ma?'

'We do.' Sandy smiles. 'But everybody is different,

Spike. People like different things; it wouldn't do for us to all be the same.'

'Why not?' Spike frowns.

'Well, because it would be a boring world to live in if we were all the same, right?'

'Suppose so.' Spike shrugs. 'You could come and live with us on *My Fair Lady*, Calum.'

'Yeah, great idea.' Amelia grins. 'Let's do it.'

'I think Calum's family might have something to say about that.' Sandy winks at me.

A few moments of silence. I realize they're all looking at me, expecting me to say something.

'I don't so much mind our flat, it's who's in it that's putting me off. I'm crawling the walls, stuck in there.'

'Is it Spiderman?' Spike's eyes are wide.

'Nah, I could cope with Spiderman, Spike.' I wrinkle my nose. 'Dad's moved his new girlfriend and her son in. I've got to share my bedroom with him.'

I wait for them to gasp in horror, say they understand how awful it must be for me.

'We have to share space in here.' Amelia shrugs. 'You get used to it and there's always room for one more.'

'Don't you like him, this boy?' Sandy asks.

'He's Polish.'

They all look back at me with blank faces.

'What's Polish?' Spike says.

'Someone who comes from a country called Poland,'

Sandy tells him. 'It's in Europe.'

'Why is he here and not in Poland then?' Spike asks.

'Exactly, Spike,' I say. 'Why's he got to live here in Nottingham, in our flat, and share my bedroom? Supposedly, it got too dangerous for them to live there.'

I roll my eyes and wait for them to tell me it's awful and they totally understand how difficult it must be for me.

But there is just silence.

I feel a heaviness in my chest and I'm suddenly worried they'll think badly of me.

'It's just that I don't want to share my bedroom with a stranger,' I say to Amelia, trying to get her on my side. 'Our flat is tiny – there's barely enough room for me and Dad as it is.'

Three pairs of eyes look away from me, down the narrow, cramped interior of *My Fair Lady*. The tiny boat that has far less space than our flat.

Through the window I can see the light is fading slightly outside. The boat is rosy and glowing inside from the hot stove and a small lamp. The cold, aching feelings I had when I left the flat have faded. I wonder briefly if that's how Sergei and his mum felt when they came to stay with us. I think about how I've just turned up here tonight and been invited inside and made to feel so welcome. How they've shared their food, drink and space with me ever since they moored on the canal.

I need something else – something to show them the unfairness of it all.

'People should live in their own homes, stay in their own places,' I add. 'What gives people the right to live on someone else's patch?'

'Are you angry we've come to live here in Nottingham, too?' Spike asks me, his eyes wide.

'Course not!' I laugh. 'It's different. I mean – you're . . . it's just different.'

'Sometimes people come here and bring much-needed skills that contribute to the economy,' Sandy says softly. 'Doesn't that make it a better place for all of us?'

'There aren't enough jobs for the people who were born here, though,' I say, pleased I've remembered something Linford is always saying. 'They can't just come over here, taking what we have. People can't just live where they like.'

'I didn't have you down as being such a prat, Calum.' Amelia stiffens in her seat. 'But now you're talking just like one.'

They all stare at me as though I just grew another head. I make my excuses, thanking Sandy for the hot chocolate, and leave.

While I'm walking back home I think about life on *My Fair Lady*. How it would feel if Sandy invited me to live with them, move on to their next place. No more suffering Sergei and his mum, having people

123

around all the time. Just family.

I think about people moving around, finding new homes, visiting new places. Like Sergei and his mum are doing, I suppose.

I don't know why I think differently about the Zurakowskis. It's like some unspoken rule says *we* have the right to live where we want and they don't. And even I have to admit that sounds pretty stupid.

★

EXT. ON BOARD *MY FAIR LADY* - DAY
A narrowboat is moored on the canal in
Newark. Official-looking MAN approaches
boat. BOY, GIRL and YOUNG BOY watch
through an open window. SANDY jumps down
from the deck to talk to him. Soon she is
gesticulating and there are raised voices.

                    MAN
     I told you, you can't stay here.

                   WOMAN
                (*frustrated*)
     But why? What harm are we doing? I find
maintenance work on boats while we're here.
We don't ask the authorities for anything.

MAN

Madam, I don't make the rules; I only
enforce them. How would it be if we let
everyone live on the river, eh? Nobody would
be able to move.

WOMAN

But not everyone wants to live on the river.
There are hundreds of miles of canals –
there's plenty of room for everybody.

MAN

As I said, I don't make the rules. You have
to move on because your permit has expired.

WOMAN

(*frowning*)

Since when did you own the water?

MAN

(*pompous tone*)

There are boundaries that must be observed,
laws that must be upheld. The canals are on
our land; they belong to the council. You
cannot live here. You must go back to where
you came from.

                    WOMAN
                  (*pleading*)
We don't have a set place to live. We travel
   around, living and working in different
                    places.

                    MAN
I'm sorry but you cannot stay here. You must
    leave. You must go somewhere else.

                    WOMAN
         Where do you suggest we go?

                    MAN
                 (*dismissive*)
      That, madam, is not my problem.

END SCENE.

16

I sleep a bit better, mainly because Sergei isn't shouting out his weird words in the night. He stays in bed a bit later this morning, too.

In my head, I keep running over the conversation I had yesterday with Amelia and her family. It's bothering me. Those things I said about people sticking to their own patch . . . I hope they don't think I mean *them* because I like having them around – they bring something new, something exciting to the canal. And I think they should be able to live where they like, not bound by silly rules and regulations.

Sergei's face pops into my mind. What's different about him and Angie coming to live here? I don't mean in our flat; I mean here, in *our country*.

It feels like they're taking something away from us just by being here and I know that doesn't really make any sense. The things that Linford says about foreigners and the headlines I've seen on the newspapers outside the shop . . . they're all swirling around in my head and it's really difficult to get past them to decide what *I* think. It just feels too hard and uncomfortable, so I push the thoughts away again.

I should've kept my mouth shut yesterday, instead of spilling my guts to Amelia, Sandy and Spike. I'd tried to change the subject but they all seemed a bit quiet after that. I did the right thing in making an excuse to leave.

After wolfing down a bowl of cereal, I grab my rucksack and head out while Sergei is still in the bathroom. When I get to the school gates there's nobody there in our usual meeting spot. Again.

I find them in the inner courtyard. I join the group and apart from a couple of grunts, nobody really says anything. A stupid tic starts up in my eye. Jack and Harry stare down at the floor as if there's something fascinating there among the new paving stones, scuffling their feet with their hands stuffed deep into their trouser pockets.

Linford, as usual, is glued to his phone.

'All right, Linford?' I say.

'Yeah, cool.'

He glances up at me and back down really quickly, but it's enough for me to spot it. A dark maroon puffiness that encircles his whole eyeball, even covering the eyelid.

My eyes flick to Harry and he holds my questioning look for a second before giving a slight shrug and looking away again. I can almost hear him hissing, *Don't ask what happened.*

'What happened?' I ask Linford.

He doesn't look up or speak. The silence seems to swell until it confines all three of us in an invisible bubble we can't seem to break out of.

'What happened?'

Linford doesn't answer me or even show he's heard me ask the question again. I glance at Jack and Harry but they won't meet my eyes and their hands burrow even further into their pockets.

Nobody speaks and somehow that just makes everything worse.

I can see Linford isn't really looking at his phone. He's just staring down at it, his fingers hovering motionless over the screen. The only thing moving is a muscle that flexes repeatedly in his jaw.

'Looks painful,' I say, looking over at Harry and Jack. They still won't look at me, but Harry's face looks scorched red.

I can feel the invisible bubble of silence pressing in closer until suddenly it bursts.

'Why don't you mind your own business?'

Linford doesn't shout or snap; his voice is calm and quiet, and somehow that makes it worse. I swallow hard and struggle to keep my voice sounding level. I feel the tic start up again in my eye.

'I just – I wondered if everything is . . .'

I think about his final warning look at me last night at his front gate and I know I can't talk to the others about it or mention what happened in front of them.

'I fell down the stairs at home, OK?' Linford shoves

his phone in his pocket and balls his fists. 'Shut your mouth about it now, I don't want to hear no more.'

When he stands up and stalks off, Jack and Harry follow him like two whipped puppies.

I watch them go and just stand where I am for a few seconds, trying to work out why what Linford just said seems out of place.

I rub at my eye, trying to make the tic stop, and then it hits me.

Linford lives with his mum, sister and stepdad in a ground-floor flat. He doesn't *have* any stairs at home to fall down.

At break-time, we don't go to the snack bar. There's more silent standing around the courtyard, Linford staring at his phone and the rest of us looking at the floor.

An incoming text beeps and Linford shields the message as he reads it. He sends a text back to whoever it is and puts his phone back in his pocket.

'I won't be coming out after school,' he says to nobody in particular, looking down. 'I've got a bit of work on.'

'What kind of work?' I ask him.

'Bits and bobs.' He shrugs. 'It pays well and that's all I'm bothered about.'

The air feels thick and warm so I loosen my tie and pull at my shirt collar but nothing seems to alleviate the stickiness.

We've all been in different lessons this morning so I haven't had a chance to ask Jack or Harry what they think about Linford's black eye, and I don't want to text them in case he sees my message. I can't even shoot them a knowing glance because neither of them will look at me. It seems to take forever for the bell to sound, but when it does, we all split for second-period lessons and, finally, I feel a bit lighter inside.

As soon as lessons break for lunch, I head straight for the Technology block, but there's nobody waiting. I wonder if the lads have had to take Linford to the school nurse to look at his eye, and nip over to the Admin block, but there is a notice on the nurse's door saying she's out for lunch.

By the time I get to the dinner hall, they are all at the front of the queue, starting to make their choices. I grab a tray and push in front of a Year Seven boy so I'm right behind Harry.

'Thanks for waiting for me,' I hiss.

'Sorry, mate, not my call.' He presses his lips together in apology and slides his tray further down the counter as the queue moves along.

I glance down the line at Linford's scowling face. I don't know when things started to change or what's making him so angry with me. After what I witnessed outside his flat, I know things aren't great at home for him, but that's hardly my fault. Maybe I could try speaking to him on his own before afternoon lessons start.

I don't feel hungry at all but I choose a tuna salad baguette and a yogurt from the counter display. My stomach feels bloated like I already stuffed far too much food down.

Usually we end up bolting our lunch at the end of our sitting because we're so busy talking and messing about instead of eating. Today, I look around our table and see the tops of three heads as everyone shovels their food in silently.

Back outside we sit on the low wall that runs around the courtyard. I slip off my blazer and look at the others. 'Anyone fancy a game of footie down the field later?'

'I thought you were too busy to play football with us these days.' Linford sniffs, banging the heel of his shoe on the floor.

'Don't be daft.' I laugh, but it catches in my throat and comes out as a cough. 'We had people coming over the other night when you asked me, that's all.'

When I think about the identity of those visitors, the palms of my hands turn instantly clammy.

'Maybe you're trying to tell us summat, Cal, like you don't want to be mates with us any more.'

'Course not!' It feels like there's a jagged piece of flint sitting right in the middle of my throat. Jack and Harry are sitting here and we're in the middle of the busy yard, but this might be the only chance I get to say my piece. 'Look, have I done something wrong? Are you mad cos I followed you home? I wish you'd just come out and say it if you've got a gripe with me.'

'What are you going on about?' Linford gives me a dark, meaningful look through narrowed eyes.

Jack and Harry look down at their feet and then up at the sky.

'I dunno, it's just that we don't seem to have such a laugh as we all used to.' I keep my voice light and relaxed, but underneath the table my toes are scrunched up tightly in my shoes.

'Yeah, well, you never want a laugh any more, do you?' Linford snaps back. 'I've seen the look on your face just lately, when we're having a bit of fun with certain people.'

By 'fun' I'm guessing he means bullying Sergei.

'You used to enjoy the craic, Cal, and now you've started acting like we're boring you. If you don't like our style then why don't you just—'

'Hey, look who it is,' Jack calls out. I could hug him for providing a distraction until I see exactly who is heading our way and who now has Linford's full attention.

'I'm sick of seeing that ignorant git,' Linford mutters behind gritted teeth. 'He's like our shadow, lately. Follows us everywhere.'

He's using his quiet, seemingly calm voice, but a grim

expression has crawled over his face. His eyebrows knot together and his jaw sets. When he stands up, his whole body is rigid.

'Come on,' I say, too brightly. 'Let's go down to the sports field now and have a kickabout.'

Nobody is listening.

I have no choice but to watch as Sergei approaches.

My body feels hot and cold at the same time and I sit down on the wall again, thinking of all the ways this terrible situation is about to get even worse.

17

Sergei's eyes are trained on mine as he walks towards us, and I look away, hoping Linford hasn't noticed.

'Yo, Immi.' Linford assumes a boxer's stance. 'You coming back for more, then?'

Sergei gets closer and then changes direction at the last second.

'Find another way to cross the courtyard, you mug,' Jack spits. 'We like breathing fresh, clean air over here.'

'I think that this is a free country,' Sergei says quietly, but carries on walking without looking at Jack. 'So I am allowed to walk in any place I choose.'

Why is it so hard for him to keep his big mouth shut?

Jack lunges at his rucksack but Sergei shrugs him off and spins round.

'Oh dear, the benefit-scrounger's got the monk on.' Harry laughs as Jack stumbles.

'My mother works every day,' Sergei replies coolly. 'So you can relax. We are not claiming any of the benefits you worry about so much.'

'She's taking someone else's job, you mean,' Linford says softly and takes a step forward. 'Someone's job who was born in this country and has earned the right to work here.'

At the start of the year, Linford told us his stepdad had been made redundant from his job at the building company where he had worked for over twenty years. Linford said that Eastern Europeans had taken all the building jobs because they were happy to work for peanuts.

But now Linford is saying all the Eastern Europeans are lazy and claiming benefits. I'm not sure which one is right, but I know it can't be both. Linford doesn't really seem to know either, and I suddenly wonder where he's getting all this information from. He's like a parrot, blindly repeating stuff that makes no sense to him or anyone else.

I think about his stepdad's angry face and how he'd seemed quite drunk when I saw him. Sometimes, I suppose, it's easier to blame other people for your problems than accept you might be making a mess of your own life.

Sergei's eyes dart over to mine but what can I do? I've warned him to stay away from us but he refuses to listen.

'Jack saw you on our estate last night,' Linford continues. 'What business you got there, you dirty scrounger? Don't tell me they've given you lot a free council flat now.'

Sergei looks at the floor.

'You might as well tell us,' Harry hisses. 'We'll find out anyway and then you'll get a brick through your window.'

They all snigger, but Sergei doesn't answer. Instead, he looks directly at me.

'What you always staring at Cal for?' Jack scowls. 'You fancy him or summat?'

He nudges me and grins, inviting me to join in with what Linford has always called our 'banter'. Except it doesn't feel like I'm included in the banter today; more like I'm on the receiving end of something more sinister . . . with Sergei.

Suddenly it doesn't seem nearly as light-hearted.

'I asked you a question, Immi,' Linford growls. 'Have you got a flat on our estate now, or what?'

Sergei looks at me one final time, his eyes pleading with me to say something, to help him out. He needs me to tell Linford the truth.

My worst nightmare is here. This is my last chance to make up a lie or a story. Otherwise, the awful truth will come out and there's nothing I can do about it.

I open my mouth. And close it again.

I can't think of anything I can possibly say that will help the awfulness of Linford's reaction when he finds out I've been lying to him about Sergei and his mum living with us.

Linford grabs the limp lapels of Sergei's blazer.

'I am living on St Matthias Road,' Sergei says, pulling away.

'That's your road, isn't it, Cal?' Jack frowns.

They all turn to look at me. Something sparks in Linford's eyes, like he's finally putting pieces of information together.

'That's why Immi is always staring at you,' Linford says slowly. 'Cos you're neighbours.'

'Not exactly,' I mutter. My school shirt is sticking to my damp armpits.

'There's only one St Matthias Road in St Ann's.' Harry frowns. 'It's *got* to be the same one you live on, Cal, so you would've seen him. You're lying, Immi.'

'He's not my neighbour.' I say the words quickly before my voices cracks and betrays me.

My insides are tangled into such a tight mess, it feels like they'll never straighten back out again.

'So, Immi *is* lying through his teeth then.' Linford moves fast and within a couple of seconds, he has Sergei by his scrawny neck and his right fist snaps back ready to strike. 'Last chance. Where do you live, you stinking little—'

'Wait!' I jump up. 'He's not lying.'

Linford's grip loosens slightly, enough for Sergei to take in a few gulps of air.

Four pairs of eyes are trained on me. Waiting for the truth.

Waiting for me to tell them what I know.

A pulsing starts up in my throat as if my heart has broken loose and has slid up from my chest.

I try my best to swallow the words back, but in the end I have no choice but to face whatever is coming. I'm just going to have to say it.

'It's our flat,' I say, and slump back down to sit on the wall. 'Sergei lives with us.'

18

Linford spins round to face me and I swallow, hard.

'I hope I just heard you wrong, Cal.'

Beads of moisture glisten on his forehead and the sharp smell of stale sweat wafts under my nose as he moves closer.

Behind him, Sergei slips away while he still has the chance. The traitor.

'You'd better explain what you mean by that.' Linford's voice comes out dangerously low. 'Are you serious? . . . Sergei Zurakowski lives with *you*?'

For a second or two, I can't speak.

A look passes between Jack and Harry and they step lightly away from Linford's side, the way they always do when he is about to hurt someone.

'The visitors that came over to ours the other night, it was them,' I babble. 'Sergei and his mum.'

'Oh man,' Harry groans, and presses the heel of his hand to his forehead.

'I didn't know.' My voice slides up an octave. 'I swear, Linford, I didn't know *who* the visitors were until I saw Sergei in our flat. It's my dad, you see, he—'

'And he never said a word,' Linford drawls slowly,

turning to the others. 'Cal's lied through his teeth to us. Traded us in for a dirty incomer, lads.'

Jack shakes his head at me in disgust.

'No . . . it's my dad, he's been dating Sergei's mum but I didn't know until the other night,' I try to explain clumsily. 'There was nothing I could do by then. I mean, tell me, what could I do about it?'

'You could've *told us.*' Harry stares at me. 'That would've been a start.'

'I was going to, honest. But Linford's been a bit –' I reach for a word – 'I don't know, *weird.* I was trying to find a good time to tell you all, I swear.'

Linford narrows his eyes.

'Calling me a weirdo now, are you?'

'No! But why does everything always have to be about *you*?' A channel of heat shoots up and into my head. I'm so sick of always treading on eggshells around Linford, I might as well just say it. I stand up. 'We always have to do what *you* like, what *you* say, and only talk to the people *you* say it's OK to talk to. It sucks.'

'You better take that back while you've still got the chance you stupid dumb—'

'We're like his puppets, all of us, right?' I spin round to Jack and Harry. They look away but I can't stop. 'He hates anyone who's different to him. Know what I think?' I turn back to Linford, my chest tight and burning. 'I think you're scared.'

Linford throws back his head and laughs. But it sounds put on, like he's acting out a stage direction.

'You think I'm *scared*?' His voice is dangerously quiet but I have to get this feeling out – it's a tightness that's been stuck inside me for ages.

'Yeah, I think you're scared. Scared of stuff that's nothing to do with school, or with the people you bully. Stuff you deal with at home that nobody else sees.'

'Cal . . .' Jack takes a step forward. 'It's just a bit of banter. Leave it.'

'It's not, though, is it?' I snap at him. 'We call it banter, but everyone else calls it bullying.'

'Quiet,' Linford growls. 'I want to hear from Cal what it is I'm *so scared* of.'

'I don't know exactly what you're scared of, Linford. I don't think you know, either.' Part of me knows I've gone too far to ever come back, and part of me feels free, like I can do or say what I want for the first time in years. 'Maybe you're scared of losing your grip here at school, scared of looking weak? All I know is, you open your mouth and your stepdad's voice and opinions fall out. You've turned into his mouthpiece.'

Jack loudly sucks in air through his teeth and steps back.

'You're dead.' Linford's face drains of colour but his eyes burn. 'You're a dead man.'

His hand clenches into a fist that's so tight I can see the bone straining through the skin on his knuckles.

142

And then I realize my own fists are clenched too. It feels weird, but for the first time in a long time, I feel like *me* again, that I'm not just Linford's puppet.

For a second, our eyes lock and I see a blip of shock flit through him.

He bites down on his back teeth and screws up his face. His fist moves back and I get ready for the blow. This is it. The end of our friendship.

The force of the blow and the crack of my jaw surprises me, sends me careering back into the wall. As I hit it, my automatic reaction is to push back and spring forward again. There's a bolt of fire channelling down my arm and I'm almost not aware my own fist is flying forward until it hits Linford squarely on the nose.

My heart feels like it's about to explode out of my chest wall and the sounds around me seem like muffled echoes in my ears. Other students are running over to catch the show and I hear whoops of amazement. My eyes refocus and I see that Linford is bent over, blood pouring from his nose.

Both Jack and Harry are looking at me like they never saw me before, their jaws hanging open.

'OK, break it up here,' a stern voice booms. 'Linford Gordon, first aid, and then my office. *Now.*' Mr Fox hands him a handkerchief.

Jack and Harry both scatter. Sergei stands in front of me with Mr Fox.

'You all right, Calum?' Mr Fox tips his head to one side, studying me sternly.

'Yes, sir,' I say, dusting down my trousers and moving my throbbing jaw from side to side. 'I'm fine.'

'If Sergei here hadn't dragged me over, I'd have said you were in line for one of Mr Gordon's trademark beatings. The ones you usually enjoy watching others suffer from the sidelines. But I saw him attack you first and it seems you've held your own on this occasion. How's the jaw?'

I wiggle my chin side to side. 'It's fine, sir.'

'Then I'll speak to you in the morning, before first lesson, please.'

'Yes, sir.'

Despite being ordered to the Head's office, Linford is still loitering behind Mr Fox, the handkerchief pressed to his nose and his dark eyes trained on to mine like he wants another go.

'It's not so good, is it, Calum, being on the other side? You're normally one of Linford's eager spectators.'

'Not any more, sir,' I say, and I mean it. I'm making my own decisions from now on. Thinking my own thoughts.

I don't see Linford for the rest of the day and there is no sign of Jack or Harry either down at the gates at the end of school.

144

I can't face going straight home today so I decide to take a detour to the Arboretum. I fold up my blazer, pull off my tie and stuff them into my rucksack.

I hope that now they've had time to think, the others can see I had no control over Sergei coming to live with us. I didn't lie to them, they have to see that.

It's about a fifteen-minute walk to get to the park and I keep looking over my shoulder, just in case Linford is out for revenge.

I rub my aching jaw. I know it's probably not over, that he'll come after me again. I feel a bit shaky at the thought of it but I'm still burning inside, too. They've all ditched me because of what's happened with Sergei and it's just stupid. I'm sick and tired of having to accept their warped rules.

As soon as I walk through the gates, my shoulders relax a little and the dryness in my mouth has got a bit easier.

They say the author J. M. Barrie got the inspiration to write *Peter Pan* here at the Arboretum, and I can see why that might be true, because today it looks a bit like a Neverland.

The Victorian flower garden is bursting with vibrant colour, and the Chinese bell tower stands regal and proud in the pale gold sunlight. It feels like I'm in a parallel universe and all the mixed-up stuff that's happening at home and at school suddenly seems far, far away.

I stand still for a moment and listen to the birds that invisibly sing in the leafy trees clumped all around me. I wouldn't mind being able to fly like Peter Pan, but I couldn't think of anything worse than never growing up. I can't wait to finish school and get a job; preferably well away from here. At the same time, I can't imagine ever being able to escape the estate.

People are born here, live here and then they die here. That's just the way things are. All the exciting things I ever hear about seem to happen to other people who have never set foot in a crummy place like this.

19

Later, when I turn the corner into St Matthias Road, I can see right away that Dad's van isn't there, thank goodness. I haven't had chance to tell Sergei to keep his mouth shut about what happened with Linford today. I just hope he's not stupid enough to blurt it out before I speak to him.

I keep everything crossed that Sergei and his mum are out, too. I really need some time to think things through.

I feel like I'm in a bubble, separate from everyone around me. All alone, even when there are people around.

As I turn the key in the flat door and push it open, my ears fill with the strains of music floating down the hallway. It sounds like the same kind of dull music that Mr Fox plays while we file into our Monday morning assemblies.

I kick off my shoes, dump my rucksack by the door and creep down the hall, looking into the rooms. It looks like Dad and Angie are out, but Sergei is holed up in my bedroom.

When I get closer, the notes are so loud and clear I spy through a crack in the door to make sure Sergei hasn't moved an actual piano into my bedroom. It wouldn't surprise me; he's filled it with all sorts of weird stuff already.

But he isn't playing the piano; he's sitting on the bed, staring into space like a zombie. His face is blank, eyes glazed over and his lips pressed together in a spongy line, like someone just blurred his features with a soft cloth.

I stand still for a moment and listen. The piano notes dance high and bright, then ping low and fast like vibrating raindrops. My heart seems to swell and then squeeze in tight on itself. I can't make my mind up whether I feel like laughing or crying.

I feel the music slowly building like a storm until finally it erupts into a twisting melody that swirls around the booming bass notes as if there is an entire orchestra stuffed into my tiny bedroom.

I close my eyes and let the music flow through me. Before I know it, my mind is drifting to a time last summer when Dad came home early unexpectedly for the weekend. We got up early Saturday morning, jumped in the van and drove for nearly three hours so we could have fish and chips for our lunch, sat on a wall in Whitby harbour.

There's a flurry of melancholy notes and another memory floats by. The day Mrs Brewster's Labrador, Frank, got knocked over in the street by a motorbike. While someone went to fetch Mrs Brewster, I sat down beside Frank in the road and cushioned his soft, velvety head in my lap until his rasping, furry chest finally lay still.

I blink hard a few times.

I don't know why I'm suddenly thinking about this stuff; it's crazy. Sergei's music is seeping into my head like a wisp of black magic, turning my sensible thoughts to mush.

The bedroom door whips open.

'Calum, why are you standing out here? Come in and listen.'

'I don't need an invite to come into my own bedroom, thanks,' I shout over the music.

I push by him and flop down on to my bed. I pick up one of my DVDs and pretend to read the blurb on the back, but the words don't make much sense.

'You were listening to the music just now.' He raises his voice above the notes.

'Waiting until it finished, more like.' I kick off my shoes without sitting up. One of them hits the small portable speaker his phone sits on and the track jumps.

'How is your jaw?'

'It's fine.' I'm trying to ignore the aching. 'So don't go blabbing to Dad about what happened this afternoon.'

'Should I turn it off, the music?'

'Please yourself.'

He reaches over and turns the volume down.

'Do you like Chopin?' He pronounces it *Show-pan*.

'What?'

'Frédéric Chopin,' he says again. 'The composer. He was born in Warsaw. This piece is called *Nocturne Number 19 in E minor*.'

I sigh, and study the cover of the DVD.

'This piece of music, it is one of his twenty-one Nocturne compositions.'

'Fascinating.' I scowl at him. 'You seem to know an awful lot about nothing.'

My insults seem to slide off him like oil.

'Chopin very quickly gets inside *here*, Calum.' He taps his heart space. 'I can see in your face that he got you, too.'

I've lost one of my best friends today because of him and his mum turning up where they're not wanted, and now he's sitting there grinning at me like an imbecile.

'Why don't you just sod off back to where you came from?'

I feel a twist inside when I realize I sound just like Linford. I half slide, half fall off my bed and kick the speaker over in the process. The music jumps, then stops completely.

'Hey, what the hell is wrong with you?' He takes a step towards me. 'You should learn some manners.'

'Oh yeah?' I glance at his clenched hands. 'And who's going to teach me some? You?'

I square up to him but the mild-mannered Sergei I

see at school isn't here. Instead I feel an undercurrent of something else coming off him and the back of my neck prickles.

'Maybe I will,' he says quietly. His eyes glitter, dark and dangerous. 'Maybe I will wait for the right moment.'

Perhaps he's just sick of tiptoeing around me, like I got fed up with Linford. I push past him.

'Yeah, right. When you're big enough,' I say when I'm at a safe distance.

I slam the door and stand for a moment in the hallway, breathing heavily.

I feel ousted from my own bedroom. How did it get to this?

Sergei seems quiet and non-confrontational at school, but here in the flat I sense a different vibe. Who knows what he is really like? What if he's leading me to believe he is harmless when really he is someone else altogether?

Sergei stays in my room all evening with the door shut.

I sit watching TV on my own in the sitting room, but I can't relax the same, knowing he's in there. I feel annoyed that he's taken over my space.

At the same time there's a thickness in my throat I can't swallow down. I get to thinking about Amelia and her family, coming to live in a new place but made to feel like impostors. I shouldn't have said some of the things

I did to Sergei. I can't really concentrate on the TV so I turn it off.

Dad and Angie still aren't back. I'm just about to flick off the lamps and go to bed when I hear shouting and whistling out on the road.

I stand still and listen and a little shiver runs down both my arms. I can't shake the uneasy feeling that now Linford will be out to get me. Dad's not here and if there's anyone out there wanting to cause trouble, they could put a brick through the window or even try and bash the door in.

I debate for a few moments whether to go over to the window. It could just be rowdies coming home from the pub, but it's still a bit early – they don't usually turn out until about eleven thirty.

Someone shouts and then there's a piercing whistle. Whoever it is seems to have stopped right outside the flat.

I walk slowly to the loosely pulled-together curtains and peer out, down on to the road. A group of about eight lads in baseball caps and hoodies are standing right outside our flat, gathered by the front gate. In the dusk, I can't make out individual faces under all the hoods and hats, but they look just like the troublemakers from the top end of the estate, the ones who were in the car that stopped outside the chippy. I've seen them roaming around like a pack of dogs before.

They look up at our window and I realize too late that with the lamps on behind me, I'm lit up like a fairy on a Christmas tree. Suddenly the group roars and points up, whistling and making unpleasant hand gestures. I'm trying to work out why they're suddenly doing that to me when I feel something touch my shoulder. I jump back to find Sergei at the side of me, staring down at the road.

'Get away from the window,' I hiss, pulling him away from the glass.

I pull the curtains back together and peer down at the road through a tiny gap at the side. As the group shuffle off slowly, still laughing and staring up, they move briefly, one by one, into light as they walk under a street lamp.

The last youth stands there a moment and glares up. I can see his top lip curling and his eyes shining with a cold fury. For a brief moment, the street light illuminates his whole face.

I step back from the gap, my heart pumping hard. It's Linford.

20

I snap awake and glance over at the red illuminated numbers on the windowsill.

It's 3.15 a.m. Sergei is snoring softly and the room is cast in a dull orange glow from the street lights.

I lie there staring at the ceiling for ages waiting for sleep to return, but every minute that passes I seem to be more awake than ever, and then my legs start to get fidgety.

I climb out of bed as quietly as I can and tiptoe past Sergei's curled-up form under the blankets of his camp bed. The last thing I want to do is wake him and then start arguing all over again.

I carefully open and close the bedroom door and pad silently into the sitting room. I look out of the window and stand for a moment to take in the quiet street. Everyone is in bed and there's no Linford glaring up at me from the front gate any more.

He might be the hard man at school but he's always stayed away from the yobs who live on the estate. Mainly because his older brother got in with the wrong crowd a few years ago and ended up having his kneecaps rearranged with a baseball bat when he tried to back out

154

of selling drugs on the streets.

I wonder if his stepdad has given him a rough time about getting excluded. Linford is a blamer, and if he's getting hassle, I bet I can guess who he's blaming right now.

I turn on the small lamp and then flick through masses of TV channels, but there's nothing on that interests me. Even the music programmes are rubbish.

And then I remember.

I creep along the hallway to the front door to get my rucksack. Dad's bedroom door is closed, so he and Angie must've managed to come home without waking me.

A few minutes later I'm lying under a blanket on the settee, watching the DVD Freya gave me. I can tell her tomorrow that I watched it, like she asked. With any luck it'll send me back to sleep.

Nearly two hours later the credits start rolling on the screen and I'm still wide awake. *Kes* might just be the best film I've ever seen.

There are no special effects, no car chases and no fighting action. It's hard to grasp why I like it so much.

I stick the DVD back in its case and into my rucksack and turn off the lamp, creeping back into my bedroom.

Sergei is still fast asleep in the exact same position as he was two hours ago. I climb back in bed and pull the covers up to my chin.

When I close my eyes, bits of *Kes* replay in my mind.

I can see Billy Casper flying his kestrel in the field.

I hear the frustration in his broad Yorkshire accent.

I feel his pain.

I wonder if Freya has any more films like that.

When I wake up, Sergei is gently shaking me. He's already fully dressed in his school uniform.

'Calum, you are oversleeping,' he hisses in my ear.

I shake him off and sit up.

'What time is it?' I scowl, trying to see past him to the clock.

'It is eight thirty-two. I have already tried to wake you two times.'

I jump out of bed and grab yesterday's school shirt off the floor.

'I will wait for you,' he says, sitting on his camp bed.

'It's OK,' I say, trying to shake the creases out of my shirt. 'I'll walk in on my own.'

He doesn't move.

'OK then,' I tut. 'Give us five minutes.'

Sergei smiles and nods. 'I overslept too – there is no time to eat breakfast. I wondered . . .'

'What?' I frown.

'There is a meeting at the community centre later today. I saw it on the noticeboard,' he says. 'About the screenwriting competition. I thought perhaps you would like to go.'

'How do you know about that?'

'I saw the flyer.' He nods down to the slightly crumpled sheet that I dropped on to the floor before going to sleep last night. 'I thought you may be thinking of entering.'

'Yeah? Well I haven't made my mind up yet,' I say, irritated.

He doesn't miss a trick, poking his nose into my business at every opportunity.

'I would go with you, just to find out a little more,' he says. 'If you would like to?'

'I'll see,' I mutter, turning my back on him.

I stuff my history textbook and the competition flyer into my bag and pull on my blazer.

I didn't know about the meeting. Maybe it would be a good idea to go. I wouldn't be committing to anything; it would just be to find out a bit more about the competition. Freya would be pleased, too.

In the kitchen I notice the fruit bowl has been cleared of all the crumpled till receipts and ballpoint pens and it's now full of fresh fruit. I take a banana and an apple and stuff those in my bag, too.

I turn to leave, then step back and take another two pieces of fruit.

'Here.' I shove the extra fruit towards Sergei in the hallway. 'We can eat these as we walk.'

'Thank you, Calum.' His mouth drops open. 'Thanks a thousand.'

'A million,' I tell him. 'You say, *Thanks a million.*'

'Thank you. Thanks a million for my breakfast.'

'Chill out, mate. It's only a bit of fruit.' I grin and he smiles back.

Jack and Harry are already in the history lesson when I get there. They're sitting right at the end of a full row of people. The row in front is empty, so I sit there, directly in front of them.

'Cheers for saving us a seat.' I turn round but neither of them answers.

At break, I follow them out of class. They stride ahead and don't wait for me.

'Hey, what's your problem?' I catch up and step in front so they have to stop walking and look at me.

'If you don't know, there's not much point us telling you,' Jack snaps back.

'It's Linford,' Harry says. 'He's been permanently excluded this time.'

'Yeah, you tosser,' Jack adds.

'How's that *my* fault?' There's something nasty curdling in my throat. I wish I could spit whatever it is out at them.

'You knew he'd do his nut when he found out you'd been lying about being friends with Sergei Zurakowski,'

Jack says, his eyes dark and narrowed. 'Mr Fox was there to see it all when he lost his temper, too. Some people might say it's like Linford walked straight into a trap.'

'I didn't lie about Sergei moving in; I just didn't know how to tell you all.' My eyes bulge with the effort of trying to make them understand. 'It all happened so quickly, it was a shock. Do you honestly think I'm happy about him being there?'

'You still should've said something,' Harry murmurs.

'I saw Linford last night,' I say quickly. 'He was hanging around on our street with that rough lot off the estate. The ones in the car outside the chippy.'

'Rubbish.' Jack shakes his head. 'He wouldn't have anything to do with those idiots. Not after his brother.'

'It was definitely him,' I say.

Nobody answers.

'Anyway, there's no need for you two to get involved in my argument with Linford.' I hear my words, strained and forced. 'We're still mates, right?'

Jack looks at me like I just farted under his nose.

'Come on, Hazza, let's go,' he says.

They walk around me.

'Soz, Cal.' Harry shrugs as he passes.

I watch as they saunter off together. They don't look back.

The rest of the classes flood out into the corridor.

Usually people are careful to walk around us, careful not to annoy us.

Today, I find myself pushed and pulled around like a feather in a storm.

Today, I feel like I'm invisible.

21

I'm walking down the hill towards the estate, debating whether to go straight home or go down to the canal, when someone shouts my name. I stop walking and turn around to see Sergei racing towards me.

'I waited for you, Calum,' he calls breathlessly. 'We can go to the community centre together. The meeting, it starts in only ten minutes.'

I'd forgotten about the meeting but I'm not really in the mood for going now anyway.

'It will be fun,' Sergei says, sensing my hesitation. 'To hear about the competition that you are going to win.'

'I don't even know if I'm entering yet.' I scowl. 'I don't need you going on at me about it.' I have enough of that from Freya.

'Calum, you *have* to enter.' He grins. 'You are so good at this stuff.'

'How would you know?' I scoff, setting off walking again. I mainly write plays in my head, so unless he's a mind reader . . .

'You seem to know a lot about films,' he says. 'That is what I mean. So, I think you could write a good script, yes? My buildings, they tell their own story, like a set design. And you tell the story through your words.'

I like the way it sounds. If only it were that simple.

By the time we get to the bottom of the hill, I've already decided not to bother going to the meeting. I don't want to sit with a load of toffs from Mapperley Top. I feel crap enough as it is, having been Nobby No Mates all day at school.

'Come on,' Sergei calls, turning into the estate as I carry on walking.

I stop and look past him, at the soft, friendly terracotta glow of the Expressions building. A woman is opening the wrought-iron gates, propping each one open. She turns and smiles at us before going back inside.

'The meeting is starting very soon,' he presses me.

There doesn't seem to be anyone around. No hordes of intelligent arty types who probably write dozens of screenplays a week.

'I am going to the meeting.' Sergei sighs. 'Will you also come, Calum?'

I am really interested in writing. I suppose there's a slight chance it might be interesting, even if I decide not to enter.

I turn around and we walk up to the community centre together.

Inside, the place is buzzing.

There are free drinks in the foyer with the dreaded

162

arty types standing together in a group, flailing their arms everywhere while they talk. I can see Hugo Fox at the centre of them, holding court and boasting about what plays he's been in. Yawn.

I notice there are also lots of people there like me. People whose eyes dart around the room nervously before looking at the floor or at their phones.

My throat feels suddenly tight and I need some air. I'm about to turn around and walk out when someone grasps my arm.

'Calum, I'm so pleased to see you here. Hello, Sergei.'

'Hello, Freya.' He beams.

'I haven't decided if I'm entering the competition yet,' I say quickly. 'He dragged me in.'

'That's absolutely fine.' She lets go of my arm and smiles at Sergei. 'This meeting is for information only. There's no obligation to enter.'

'That is what I told him, Freya.' Sergei nods. 'It will give Calum information about the competition and be interesting for him.'

'Exactly.' Freya smiles. 'Well done, Sergei!'

Sergei is such a creep. Talking about me to Freya as if I'm a little kid.

'Yeah, well, like I said,' I mumble. 'I've not made my mind up yet.'

'OK, well I'll catch up with you afterwards, see what you think,' Freya says, spotting someone else she knows and drifting away from us.

Getting the hard sell about the competition from Freya isn't my idea of fun. I'll be making a quick exit after the meeting.

'I will get us some juice and a biscuit,' Sergei says, and walks over to the refreshment table.

'Fancy meeting you here,' someone whispers in my ear.

I spin round to come face to face with Amelia. Her face is so close to mine I can see her long lashes and a sort of dancing light in her enormous brown eyes.

'What are you doing here?' I step back, wishing I hadn't got my crumpled school uniform on.

Amelia is wearing white denim shorts and a white T-shirt, paired with her usual Converse trainers that she somehow makes look stylish, rather than low-key. I glance at her slim brown legs and smooth arms, before looking away.

'Pleased to see you here, too.' She grins. Against her pink glossy lips, her teeth seem even whiter today. 'I often come up here. They have some good events on.'

'Are you entering the screenwriting competition?' I ask, willing my cheeks to cool down a bit.

'Me? Oh no, that's not my sort of thing. I come to all sorts of stuff here though, just to get off the boat, you know? For something to do.'

Sergei appears with two white plastic cups of orange

squash and two chocolate bourbons clutched in one grubby hand.

'Who's this, then? Your friend?' Amelia is as forthright as ever.

'His name's Sergei,' I grunt, taking a cup from him. 'This is Amelia. She lives on a narrowboat moored on the canal.'

'Hello, Sergei!' Amelia holds out her hand. 'I remember now, Calum told us all about you when he visited, how pleased he is you're staying with him.'

I glare at her but she won't look at me.

'I am very pleased to meet you, Amelia.' Sergei hastily hands me the biscuits and wipes his fingers on the side of his school trousers before reaching for Amelia's hand.

She snatches it back before he can grasp it. 'The trick that never gets old!' she squeals.

I scowl.

Sergei roars with laughter. 'Aha, you got me that time, Amelia. Good one!'

I look at him, surprised. He seems to be suddenly picking up some English phrases.

'Sorry, mate.' Amelia grins and shakes his hand properly this time. 'I'm a sucker for it, aren't I, Calum?'

I shuffle my feet and take a sip of my juice.

'I like people who are fun,' Sergei beams. 'And living on a narrowboat, that sounds a lot of fun. My home city, Warsaw, sits on the Vistula River. It is the longest and largest river in the whole of Poland and we see a lot of boats on there.'

'Cool!'

'And near my home, there was a big boatyard, too. I really like all types of boats.'

Sergei is such a bragger. I can tell Amelia is impressed by the way she's nodding and widening her eyes as if what he's saying is really interesting. He's so annoying.

Someone claps their hands over the other side of the foyer. It's the woman I saw opening the gates.

'Hi, everyone, thanks for coming. Can you take your seats in the hall now please, we're about to start.'

Everyone begins to filter through into the big space in the middle of the centre.

'I will get you a juice to take through, Amelia,' Sergei says and disappears.

'Your friend is *such* a gentleman.' Amelia's eyes dance around my glum face and she presses her lips together as if she's trying to stop herself from laughing out loud. 'Maybe you could learn something from him, instead of calling him names behind his back.'

'I haven't said anything I wouldn't say to his face.' I wish I could take back what I said about Sergei and his mum on the narrowboat, but I'm not grovelling to Amelia when she's in this mood.

'Well you should be ashamed then. Is it really too much to ask, to welcome new people and offer a bit of support? Some friend you are to him.'

'I never said he was my friend,' I growl, watching as the foyer empties around us.

'No? Why are you with him then?' She nudges my arm, goading me.

'I can't get rid of him.' I clench my back teeth together.

Sergei springs back in front of Amelia, holding up her juice like an eager puppy.

'Thanks, Sergei,' she says with a smile. 'Calum was just saying how you two are such good friends now.'

'We have some work still to do, I think.' Sergei glances doubtfully at me. 'But one day, we will arrive there.'

I turn round and start walking into the hall. My head is starting to pound and I feel hot.

I can hear Amelia laughing behind me.

22

The meeting was good. Informal, but with lots of information and tips on screenwriting.

Secretly I'm glad Sergei persuaded me to go. I can feel the pleasant buzz of new ideas inside my head. They're flitting back and forth, mixed in now with a bit of confidence and hope. I wonder how long it will last before I'm telling myself I can't do it again.

When we leave the centre, it is still early.

'Fancy a walk down to the canal?' Amelia says. 'Sergei could come and see *My Fair Lady*.'

'I would very much like to see your thin boat, Amelia,' Sergei says as if he's properly honoured.

'You mean *narrow*boat.' I roll my eyes at him.

'No, I like that, Sergei,' Amelia says, grinning. 'You're redesigning the English language and doing a great job of it.'

They both laugh and I can't help joining in because 'thin boat' does sound quite funny.

We walk for a while in companionable silence and soon we reach the canal side and there she is, *My Fair Lady*, in all her brightly painted splendour.

Nobody is home, so Amelia unlocks the cabin doors

with her long key and we step inside.

'You have a beautiful home, Amelia.' Sergei smiles and his eyes look distant. 'It is warm and has cosiness in the air.'

'Cosy,' I tell him. 'You just say it's *cosy*.'

'Ah yes, it is warm and cosy. As our little house in Warsaw used to be, before . . .'

He leaves the sentence hanging and Amelia glances at me.

'He didn't want to leave,' I tell Amelia, to save Sergei explaining. 'But he had to. They had . . . well, problems – didn't you, Sergei?'

'Hmm,' he says, staring at the wood-burner at the end of the galley. 'Problems.'

'Well, the good thing about problems is that they can be overcome,' Amelia says lightly, pulling out a pack of chocolate biscuits from behind a small, gathered curtain. 'We had problems too, in our old house. Even though there were lots of different nationalities in my class, I got bullied after school by the kids who lived next door to us.'

'*You* got bullied?' I repeat. I can't imagine anyone bullying Amelia.

'Yeah, they were three years older than me, didn't like the way my skin was a different colour to theirs. Their dad had been in prison for football hooliganism and he thought it was funny when they openly abused other kids.'

'What happened?' Sergei asks.

'Mum complained to the school and they both got excluded. But then horrible stuff got painted on the door, rubbish dumped in the garden, but nobody had ever seen anything because other neighbours were scared of the family. You get the picture – it wasn't nice. I was so relieved when Mum said we were going to start a new life, on the water.'

'You never told me any of that before,' I say faintly.

'You never asked,' she replies.

Later, when I get into bed, I lie awake for ages.

My legs feel restless and fidgety as my head swirls with ideas of what I might write for the competition. I start to think about Amelia and what she told me about her problems, back where they used to live.

★

EXT. SCHOOL GATES - DAY
School bell is ringing. Children rushing
towards gates, laughing and chatting among
themselves.

A TALL GIRL sticks close to the wall and
keeps her head low. She is alone.

A BOY and a GIRL approach her. They look
around, check nobody is watching.

GIRL
(*taunting*)
Ugh, look who it is. Our stinking neighbour.

BOY
Why do you live in this country? Your skin
is made for the hot weather.

TALL GIRL keeps walking out of the school
gates and doesn't look at her tormentors.
The BOY pushes her hard against a hedge.

BOY and GIRL laugh. GIRL pulls at TALL
GIRL's hair ribbons.

GIRL
You don't deserve pretty things. You're dark
and ugly. You should put a bag on your head.

BOY
(*aggressively*)
We hate you. We hate living next door to you
and your family.

GIRL
You don't belong here.

171

TALL GIRL arrives home. She goes straight upstairs to her bedroom and closes the door. She sits and looks out of the window, at the trees waving slightly in the breeze.

She wonders why the neighbours hate her.

She dreams of a better place, near the water. A friendly place.

END SCENE.

23

The next morning I wake first, so I gently shake Sergei's shoulder as I walk past.

He comes into the kitchen while I'm eating a bowl of cereal.

'I didn't know what you fancied for breakfast but I poured you some orange juice,' I say.

'Cool,' he says.

I look at him.

'What is wrong?' he asks.

'When did you start speaking like that?'

'Like what? You mean like you?' He grins. 'I listen and learn, Calum.'

When I finish eating I put the cereal away and the milk back in the fridge. There's juice, eggs, cheese, yogurts, milk . . . and they're all *fresh*. Since Angie took over the food shopping, I've never seen our fridge so full.

While we walk to school I tell Sergei what I heard about Linford yesterday.

'So he won't be coming back to the school?' Sergei gasps. His face brightens.

'That's right,' I say. 'He'll have to find another school to take him. His stepdad will do his nut.'

Sergei doesn't reply at first; I can tell he's thinking.

'But Linford knew Mr Fox would exclude him if he acted in a violent way,' he says simply. 'Is this correct?'

'Well, yeah. I suppose so but . . .' I'm not sure what I'm trying to say. 'Sometimes people get excluded when they haven't even done anything wrong. Like me.'

'But you were part of Linford's gang, Calum.'

'*I* didn't do anything wrong though, did I?' I snap back. I'm beginning to regret walking in with him now. 'I've never bullied anyone.'

Sergei sighs heavily and shakes his head. I wait for him to come back with his lame arguments, but he doesn't.

We're about halfway up Woodborough Road when an old Jack Russell ambles by. I recognize him as the dog of an old guy who walks him every morning along here. He lets the dog run ahead a little so I know he won't be far away.

'Watch this,' Sergei says. He walks towards the dog and kicks his foot at the animal. His kick falls too short, and the dog, sniffing the pavement, doesn't even realize he's there. 'I missed this time. Watch again.'

'Oi!' I rush up behind him and pull him back. 'What're you doing, you tosser? Don't kick him!'

Sergei shrugs me off and carries on walking up the hill.

'What did you do that for? What's that poor dog ever done to you?' I shove him but he doesn't look at me.

He smiles. *Smiles!*

'Don't worry, Calum,' he says. '*You* did not try to kick the dog, so nobody will blame you.'

'That's not the point. I'm not just going to stand by and watch while you hurt an innocent animal,' I yell at him. 'What kind of person do you think I am?'

He doesn't say anything. He just looks at me, nods and then smiles again.

And then I get it.

I understand what he is trying to tell me.

I walk across the courtyard to the Admin block. I don't see Jack or Harry at the school gates or in assembly. If I'm honest, I don't really care any more.

Word has got around that Linford has been excluded and that there is trouble between the three of us because of it.

Earlier, I sat through Mr Fox's assembly on my own, listening to the whispers behind me, and later I noticed the nudges and sly grins when everyone moved to their first lesson. The other students suddenly seem way more confident, bumping into me on purpose and refusing to move out of the way when the crowd bulges at the exit doors.

Finally I break through and take in a gulp of fresh air, jostled as everyone pushes past. I turn to my left and head for the Admin block, the opposite direction to everyone else, who are all heading for lessons. I knock at Freya's office door and wait, relieved to be away from everyone's prying eyes for a little while.

The door opens immediately and Freya's scrubbed, beaming face appears. She is wearing purple-and-yellow floral leggings with a brilliant-white T-shirt.

I feel dowdy next to her.

'Calum, come in.' She stands aside so I can enter. 'Lucky for me, I get to see you three times this week!'

I sit down in my usual seat. The room feels stuffy and warm.

'Have you managed to write anything else in your journal?' She sits opposite me and pours the water.

'I did, but I left my notebook at home, miss,' I lie. 'Sorry.'

'No worries. But try and write a little in your journal each day over the holidays, get those thoughts down.'

I nod. There is still a poster on her wall with the phrase 'SAY NO TO BREXIT' splashed across it.

'Were you interested in the Brexit debate, Calum?' Freya follows my eyes.

'No. I don't know anything about it, really,' I say, and the thoughts I'd tried to push to the back of my mind – why I feel it's OK for Amelia to choose to live here but not Sergei – loom large in my head again. 'I don't know what to think.'

'There's a lot of noise out there, isn't there?' Freya sighs. 'Hard to know who to listen to at times.'

'Yes, miss, that's just it. What do you think about it? You know, immigration and stuff.'

'Well, I'm all for it, but I suppose I *would* say that, right?' She laughs but I don't get it. 'Being Irish?' she adds.

'Oh yes, I see . . .' I nod.

'Some people say we are *all* immigrants. That if you go back far enough, everyone has someone of a different nationality in their family tree. It's a big world and I like to think it belongs to all of us. But of course, some people think differently.'

I nod slowly. 'Some people think they're just coming to take our jobs and claim benefits.'

'It's true that some people say that,' Freya replies. 'But other people say our NHS would collapse if it wasn't for the EU nationals who work in it.'

'I didn't know that,' I say, surprised.

'There are always two sides to any debate, and I always try and find out what they are before making my own mind up.' Freya smiles.

I consider this. It sounds a sensible approach.

'So, are you looking forward to the summer break?' She claps her hands in front of her and sits back.

I shrug.

'What've you got planned?'

'Maybe working away with my dad,' I say, taking a sip of water.

It might be fun to pretend the summer is going to be exciting, with lots of activities and things to do. Give us something to talk about.

'Sounds interesting,' she says, smiling.

'Well, that's what I wanted to do but it might not happen now.' I snap my mouth shut before anything else can spill out.

'R-i-i-ight.' Freya says it slowly and watches me. It feels like I'm supposed to say more.

'Dad's got a new girlfriend and she's just moved in.' I'm trying to act as if I'm cool about it all, but I can feel my jaw clenching. 'Her son has moved in as well.'

'And how do you feel about that?'

'I don't like it,' I say quickly, looking at my hands. 'But nobody listens to what I want.'

'It's hard when other people seem to make all the decisions in our lives,' Freya offers. 'Frustrating.'

I nod.

'I've got to share my bedroom with her son.' I bite down on my tongue to try and shut myself up, but the words just keep on spitting out like bitter pips. 'He thinks he knows everything about everything, but really he knows nothing.'

'I see,' Freya says.

I'm not going to tell her it's Sergei Zurakowski. For

all I know, he's probably already told her all about it in his own counselling sessions. Made it all my fault, so she feels sorry for him.

'Maybe you should tell your new room-mate some things that *you* know about, Calum. Even things up a bit.'

I let out a short, hard laugh. 'Like what?'

'Well, I'm sure you write very well and I know you're interested in crafting screenplays.'

A flush of heat encircles my neck.

'Did you manage to watch the film I gave you?'

'Yeah,' I mumble. I reach into my rucksack and hand it to her. 'Thanks.'

She takes the film but keeps her eyes on me.

'And what did you think of it, the film?'

"'S'all right,' I say.

She doesn't say anything.

I can hear the clock ticking on the wall above me and a telephone starts ringing in the reception area outside.

'It was good,' I add. 'Really good.'

She perks up. 'I'm so pleased. It's one of my favourites.'

Her face looks alive. She's thinking about the scenes in *Kes*.

'I like it when Billy writes that piece in class,' I say, rubbing at a mark on my trousers. 'And when he flies the kestrel in the field and his teacher comes to watch. I like that scene, too.'

'So do I, Calum.' Freya nods. 'Is it the first independent film you've watched?'

'I think so,' I say. 'I usually watch thrillers and stuff with car chases in.'

'I like those too.' Freya smiles. 'But a film like *Kes*, well, it goes a bit deeper, you know?'

'It makes you feel stuff inside,' I murmur.

'Exactly. It stirs the emotions. What did you think of the characters?'

'Dunno really, they're just ordinary, like the people on our estate, I suppose. They've got real-life problems and most of them haven't got much money.'

'Spot on.' Freya nudges forward on her seat and clasps her hands together. 'See, Calum, that's what makes a film like *Kes* so powerful. Its authenticity.'

'Yeah.' I look down at my hands again. 'It feels real. Like the stories my grandad used to tell me about his life. They were always about ordinary, everyday things, but I loved hearing them.'

Freya nods slowly.

'So, when we have a conversation about writing something for the Expressions competition and you tell me that nobody would be interested in the people or the things that happen around here, I think about a film like *Kes*, or your grandad's stories, and it blows your argument right out of the water.'

'Yeah . . .' I look up and give her a little smile.

'You've got a lot to say Calum, a lot to offer.' She taps her chest. 'If you can get what you feel in here down on paper, you will have something very special indeed. Something worthwhile.'

'I might give it a go then,' I say, and at least for the short time I'm in Freya's office, entering the competition actually feels like it might be achievable.

24

For the first time ever since I started this school, I spend my lunch hour in the library.

We have regular study sessions in here with Mr Ahmed, but I know Jack and Harry never come in during their own time unless they're forced, so I should be able to keep out of their way for a short time.

I spot Sergei sitting at a table alone in the History section. He raises his hand and nods at the spare chair on his table to indicate it's free.

This is where he must have been coming every day after the lunch hall – the one place he can be sure of not bumping into Linford, Jack or Harry. Or me, I suppose.

I shake my head and move over to the Fiction section and sit on a stool at the long, narrow bench that runs along the wall. I'm still miffed at him for pulling that stunt with the dog this morning. And I feel uncomfortable facing what it taught me about myself.

Mr Ahmed, the librarian, walks by, carrying a stack of books and does a double-take.

'Nice to see you in here, Calum,' he says, coming over. He glances at the bare desk in front of me. 'Looking for a good read?'

'Nah,' I say. 'I'm just going to do a bit of homework in here, thanks, sir.'

'OK, are you reading anything interesting at the moment?'

I shake my head. I wish he'd just leave me alone.

'Well, be sure to give me a shout if you want any recommendations. I've just had a batch of new releases in.'

He's already moving away when a thought pops in my head.

'Have you got a copy of *Kes* in here, sir?'

He turns round and smiles.

'Ah, a classic film. The original book is called *A Kestrel for a Knave*, written by Barry Hines. Did you know that?'

'No, sir.'

'Wait here a moment,' he says.

Two minutes later Mr Ahmed is back and hands me a paperback with a photo of Billy Casper on the cover. Except in this picture he's not sticking two fingers up; he is holding his kestrel. Billy looks fierce and proud, just like his bird, Kes.

'Make sure you sign it out before you take it, and don't forget, I'm opening up the library to students on Tuesday and Thursday lunchtimes during the holidays, so feel free to pop in at any time.'

'Yes, sir, thanks.'

'Lots more books here like that one if you enjoy it,'

he says before walking away.

I trace my finger over the title letters before I open the book and read a bit about the author.

Barry Hines was born in a mining village near Barnsley in Yorkshire. His first job was as an apprentice mining surveyor.

I'm stunned he wasn't a posh, educated writer from London. No mention of Hollywood or his parents being publishers or professors. He sounds just like an ordinary bloke.

'Calum!'

I jump up and snap the book closed.

Sergei glances at it and then sits down on the stool next to me.

'What do you want?' I scowl, annoyed at the interruption.

'I wondered if you would like to walk home together after school,' he says. 'I know you are angry about the dog. But I would never have kicked him, you know.'

'You shouldn't have even faked it,' I say.

'I wanted to show you, to make you see—'

'Yes. I know,' I snap, sliding off the stool. 'I know what you were telling me, OK? I get it.' I walk towards the library desk and look back at him. 'I'll meet you at the school gates, end of school, OK?'

Sergei nods and grins and heads off.

'So, have you seen the film adaptation of this book, Calum?' Mr Ahmed asks as he scans its bar code.

'Yes, sir, and I really enjoyed it.'

'I might just watch it myself again over the summer. It brings back many happy memories of Yorkshire for me.'

'Did you used to live in Yorkshire then, sir?'

'Oh yes, I grew up in Barnsley, where *Kes* is set.' He looks at the book cover and smiles to himself. 'That's where we settled when I came to the UK from Pakistan with my parents. I was just three years old. I came to Nottingham to do my university degree and I've stayed here ever since.'

So, that makes Mr Ahmed . . . *an immigrant*?

'Don't look so surprised, Calum,' he says with a grin.

'I'm not, sir. I mean, I just thought you were born here, I didn't know that you were . . .'

I don't want to upset Mr Ahmed, so I just shut up. I feel my cheeks heat up and he smiles as if he somehow knows what I'm thinking.

'I'm glad you're here, anyway, sir,' I manage. 'We wouldn't have such a good library here if you weren't.'

Mr Ahmed laughs.

'I like to think of this country as a giant library.' He sweeps his arm to take in the shelves of books surrounding us. 'Lots of different genres and stories make for an interesting place to be. Not so much fun if we only stocked one sort of book. Don't you agree?' He smiles and holds out *A Kestrel for a Knave*.

'Yes, sir, I suppose you're right. I've never thought of it like that.' I take the book and push it into my rucksack.

It's mine now for the whole summer.

After school I hang around a bit near the gates, waiting for Sergei to appear.

Part of me hopes to catch Jack and Harry before they leave, too. It's my last chance to see them before the holidays.

I want to try explaining my side of things again in the hope we might patch things up, arrange to play footie on the field at the weekend or something.

I stand behind the gatepost, just out of the crush of the crowds that surge forward. Year Eleven leavers, their shirts covered in coloured pen marks and signatures of students and staff, lope past me, excited to be walking out of the gates for the last time as schoolkids.

A group of girls shuffle past, arms around each other like a giant rugby tackle. Some are crying, but some have sparkling, hopeful eyes at the thought of being free of this place.

The crowds thin out into narrow streams of regular students and then, finally, just a few stragglers and people waiting for lifts.

No Sergei. No Jack or Harry.

I walk home the long way even though it feels like it might rain. Part of me would quite like to get soaked to the skin just to feel fresh again. But deep down, I know it'll take more than a few raindrops to wash away my problems.

When I reach the bottom of the hill and turn into the estate, I stop outside the Expressions building.

The shutters are down but details of the competition are still fixed to the fancy railings. I peek behind the poster at the plastic wallet and see that most of the copies giving entry details have gone. Probably loads of people will enter it, people who are really good writers and watch all the right sort of films.

A sharp movement near the bins grabs my attention and instead of pressing my face to the railings to see more, I step back to the edge of the pavement so I can see past the bins that are clustered together.

'Hey!' I call. 'Who's there?'

And that's when I hear it.

The growl of a souped-up engine, and loud, thumping music with a heavy bass beat.

I look up and down the road to see where the noise is coming from but can't see anything. I hear shouting voices, like an argument. Someone sounds really angry.

Then I hear doors slamming.

I step back off the pavement and into the road so I can see around the slight bend at the end of the street.

For a few seconds, the road goes quiet again, with just the faint hum of traffic on Huntingdon Street behind me. Next thing, there's an excruciating screech of tyres, powerful engine revs, and a blur of black metal hurtles towards me.

In that split-second I register that I need to move, and I throw myself back on to the pavement, thinking I've just managed to make it before the vehicle reaches me.

That's when I feel an immense jolt and a searing pain that envelops my legs and hips. Loud, thumping music fills my ears and I squeeze my eyes shut as a massive silver grille screeches to a halt, level with my face.

I open my eyes.

My cheek presses against the rough, cool surface of the pavement.

The vibration of feet pounds nearby and a tall shadow looms over me. I look at the trainer that is right next to my face. Something glistens on the leather but I can't keep my eyes focused long enough to process what I'm looking at.

Sounds, colours, smells . . . they're all merging into a senseless fog of nothingness.

Someone gasps out loud.

I hear people talking, then shouting, but the words float by just out of my grasp and I can't understand anything that is being said.

Then . . . quick movements.

Feet scuffle close to my head, car doors slam. An engine roars, and suddenly I am alone and it is deathly quiet and the daylight seems too searingly bright.

I close my eyes and the bass beat fades away, far into the distance.

I am lost in a blanket of silence.

And then the whole world turns black.

25

When I open my eyes, Dad is sitting next to me. I'm in a strange bed.

The unfamiliar room is sparse and painted white. I can smell disinfectant and cooked cabbage.

'Calum!' Dad jumps up and presses a buzzer. I grimace as the sound reverberates in my ears. 'Thank God you're OK.'

I open my mouth to speak but my throat is so dry and my lips feel so cracked, the only sound that comes out is a croaking noise.

I remember lying in the road and the feeling of a cool roughness under my cheek.

I remember the booming bass beat.

I remember the sound of scuffling feet.

Of people running.

My legs pulse with a dull, throbbing pain that feels like the worse toothache ever, but deep down in my all bones.

'You got knocked down in the street, Calum; it was a hit-and-run,' Dad says softly. 'The bloody cowards mounted the pavement. If I could get my hands on them I'd—'

'I'll just take his blood pressure, Mr Brooks,' a nurse says brightly, wheeling a tall contraption over to the bed. 'Glad you're back with us, Calum. You gave us all quite a scare.'

The croaking noise escapes my mouth again.

'You can give him a sip of water if you like,' she says to Dad, and straps a black padded cuff to my upper arm.

Dad looks pleased to be given a job to do. He jumps up and picks up the water jug and pours some into a plastic cup. He supports the back of my head and I manage to take a couple of tiny sips.

The water is warm and I can taste chlorine, but at least it's wet and trickles down the back of my throat, easing the dry soreness a little.

I point to the cup again and Dad helps me take another few sips.

'Thanks.' A raspy voice emerges from my throat.

'Do you know why you're in hospital, Calum?' the nurse asks. The black cuff inflates and tightens, pinching at my arm. 'Can you remember what happened yesterday?'

Yesterday? It feels like I just closed my eyes in the road a few seconds ago and woke up again here.

Dad's already told me about the hit-and-run but I can remember bits of it myself.

'Knocked over,' I manage to whisper. 'Loud music.'

'The police want to speak to you as soon as you feel

up to it,' Dad says, watching my face. 'Nothing to worry about, but these people need catching before they mow down anyone else. Did you see who was driving the car?'

The nurse holds up a hand. 'Go easy on him, Mr Brooks. It's a lot to take in when he's only just opened his eyes.'

Dad looks sheepish and shuts up.

I can't remember the car hitting me and I can't remember seeing the driver.

I only remember the sounds and how it felt to be lying as weak as a kitten, in the gutter, all alone.

Dad stays with me all day.

He keeps nipping down to the hospital cafe and bringing food back up, which he eats in my room. I can't eat the hospital food but Dad seems to love it.

I nibble a couple of bits of dry toast but I don't feel hungry at all.

Everything disappears behind the ceaseless throbbing in my hips, thighs and even my feet. It's all I can think about. I feel smaller, somehow. Smaller and quieter, as if I'm taking up less space in the world and life is carrying on all around me.

'You've got to eat, Calum,' Dad says, his mouth full of ham and cheese sandwich. 'You've got to keep up your strength.'

It doesn't feel like there is any strength left in my body *to* keep up.

After tea, the doctor does his rounds. The nurse says I'm one of the first patients on his list.

Another nurse comes to the door and makes a sign to Dad. He steps out of the room for a minute and then he is back. With two policemen.

'These officers want a really quick word, Calum,' Dad says. 'Nowt to worry about, lad.'

The officers' uniformed importance seems to fill the whole room. It feels like I'm the one that did something wrong.

'Hello, Calum,' the bald one says. 'I'm PC Bolton and this is my colleague, PC Channer.'

PC Channer has bright red hair and a face so full of freckles I can hardly see any plain skin. He nods to me.

'Hello,' I croak.

'We need to catch these lowlife wasters,' Dad rages. 'We can't have our kids being mowed down in the street outside the place that's supposed to be the safe heart of our community. I feel like finding them myself and—'

'Calm down, Mr Brooks, please.' PC Bolton holds up his palm to Dad. 'We have every confidence we'll apprehend the culprits, but we have a procedure to follow. Now, if we can press on with speaking to Calum?'

'Yes, course.' Dad's face reddens. 'Sorry.'

They ask me a lot of questions, most of which I'm unable to answer.

Did I see the vehicle?

No, I just heard the music.

What was the music?

I don't know, just a heavy bass beat.

Did I see the driver or anyone at all?

No, but I heard them talking, and one of them stood next to me and I saw his trainer.

Can you describe the trainer?

No, I can't remember any details.

How many of them were there?

I don't know.

What did they say?

Sorry, I don't know.

PC Bolton frowns, tucking his notepad away in his top pocket.

'Sorry,' I say again.

Dad looks disappointed when PC Channer hands him a card. 'Give us a call if and when your son remembers anything, sir.'

While Dad shows them out and they talk in low voices outside the door, I stare out of the window and wish I could fly away from here.

It looks like whoever did this is going to get away with it. No witnesses – at least none who are prepared to come forward – no memory of the accident from me, and no apparent clues.

It's like someone just committed the perfect crime.

*

Dr Hall is tall and thin with black slicked-back hair and pointed, shiny shoes. He looks more like a scientist who works at a top-secret government lab than an NHS doctor. He sweeps into the room surrounded by medical students in flapping white coats who frown at me briefly and then scribble stuff down on their clipboards.

'Your leg got knocked up pretty badly,' he says, flicking through the papers on the clipboard that is tethered with string to the end of my bed. 'Lots of pins in there now, helping you to heal. Hope you're not planning on going through the airport scanners any time soon.'

Him and Dad share a chuckle.

'We'll keep you dosed up on painkillers, but the good news is, you didn't sustain a head injury so you can go home tomorrow. The hospital will lend you a wheelchair.'

'A wheelchair?'

Dad opens a bag of crisps and shovels a handful into his mouth.

'It won't be forever,' the doctor chides me, replacing the clipboard. 'Just for a couple of days, most likely, then you'll be fine on crutches for short distances. You've been lucky this time.'

'Thanks, Doc,' Dad says gravely.

'The whole summer?'

'Oh, look who's here.' Dad stands up and wipes his greasy hands down the front of his jeans. 'We've got visitors, Calum.'

I turn my aching head gingerly towards the door and watch as Angie and Sergei move aside to let the doctor and his entourage out, then step fully into the room themselves.

Angie bends her knees, pulls a cartoon face and wiggles her fingers at me in a silly wave.

'How is our little soldier feeling?' she says in her heavy, flat accent. 'I hear you will be at home all summer. We can bake and read, and Sergei will take you to the park in your wheelchair.'

I close my eyes and count to five in the hope I'm hallucinating and have just created this nightmare scenario in my head. But when I open my eyes, Sergei is standing right next to me, and now my skull, as well as everything else, is throbbing.

'We can build my models all summer,' he says. 'And I can play you all of Chopin's Nocturnes.'

'Hear that, Calum?' Dad claps a hand on to Sergei's shoulder and looks at me hopefully. 'You two lads are going to have a brilliant time together.'

The three of them stand grinning at me as if me being knocked over is the best thing that could have happened.

'I think I'm going to be sick,' I croak, and Dad grabs a cardboard dish and holds it under my chin.

When Angie and Sergei have gone to the cafe, I push the dish away. Dad passes me a cup of water and I take a tiny sip.

'When are they going back to Poland?' I croak. 'They might *have* to go back, when Brexit goes through.'

Dad squints at me like the sun is shining straight into his eyes.

'Nah, that won't happen,' he says after a pause. 'I'm not interested in all that political rubbish anyway.'

He wafts my comment away with a flick of his fingers and I know the subject is closed.

'I liked it when it was just us two at home,' I say. 'I miss it.'

'I know things have changed, but that's not so bad, is it?' Dad tries to reason.

I shrug. I can tell I'm on to a loser; I might as well stay quiet.

'Angie's already fond of you, and Sergei's a great lad, isn't he?'

He's stopped squinting now but the corners of his mouth are drooping.

'I don't want you to grow up like me, Calum; I want different for you. Family matters – it gives you a solid base, you know?'

'We already *are* a solid base . . .' I bite my lip. 'You and me.'

Dad sighs and looks down. 'I've failed you a bit, lad, I think. Working away so much.'

'It's never bothered you before.' I feel a stab of annoyance inside. 'How come you're suddenly so concerned?'

197

Dad looks at me in a way that makes me immediately feel sorry for being so blunt.

'I don't blame you for being hacked off with me, lad; it's no more than I deserve.' Dad looks out of the window. 'It's Angie, you see. She was shocked when I told her you'd had to fend for yourself during the week.'

''S'all right.' I shrug, feeling like a little kid. 'I cope OK.'

Dad shakes his head.

'There's no two ways about it. You spent far too much time on your own in that flat. You need to be around people. Family and friends.'

Like Angie and Sergei? I don't think so.

'And I've made a bit of a decision.' Dad puffs his chest out. 'I've decided I'm going to make a real effort to be around a bit more over the summer.'

I look at him.

'I mean it, Calum. I'm going to turn down work abroad, if I have to. Now this has happened –' he nods to my shattered leg under the blanket – 'it's time for me to buck my ideas up and be a proper father to you.'

I've heard Dad's promises before and they've never come to much so far.

Suddenly I feel so tired I could sleep for a week. My eyelids seem to be made of lead and it's hard to keep them open. After a few seconds, I give in and close them.

I don't realize I've drifted off into sleep until I hear

Dad's trainers squeak on the floor as he creeps out of the room. He closes the door behind him.

He'll have gone to the cafe to be with *them*.

My legs are throbbing worse now. I need my next lot of painkillers, but Dad's gone and I've nobody else here to look after me.

My nose feels blocked; maybe I'm getting a bad cold. I feel a warm trickle at the side of my face as a tear escapes and traces its way down towards my ear. I turn my head to the small window so the pillow soaks up the moisture and I squeeze my eyes tight to seal the other tears in.

Outside I see Dad, Angie and Sergei walking across the car park, talking and laughing together. They look like a proper family just as they are, without me.

I've always been all right on my own. I learned a long time ago how to avoid other people finding out I'm by myself a lot in the flat. Now, I wish I had people around me. People who care. Being a loner only works when you don't feel down. But Angie and Sergei aren't the people I want.

I try to swallow down the sour taste in my mouth.

Why am I suddenly thinking about how different things would be if Mum was still here?

26

On Sunday morning, everyone turns up at the hospital to take me home.

'There was no need for you all to come,' I say, frowning, when they appear at the door. I wish Dad had just come on his own.

'We are here to support you, Calum,' Angie says. 'That is what family and friends do, yes?'

But Angie and Sergei aren't family, and I don't really know them enough to call them friends. But I know they mean well.

Dad pulls in a wheelchair from the corridor and unfolds it. I push the bedclothes to one side and swing my legs round.

A searing pain shoots from my toes into my hip and I cry out. Dad reaches forward as if to grab me.

'Pete, wait. Perhaps the nurse should be here.' Angie ducks out of the door and I'm grateful when she returns ten seconds later with a male nurse. Dad's trying his best to help, but he's got no sense at times.

'No aerobics classes for a few weeks, young man,' the nurse quips as he ducks under my armpit and takes my weight on to his shoulder. 'And no more wrestling classes for at least a year, OK?'

Dad, Angie and Sergei all laugh and so I feel under pressure to give him a tiny smile, but really I'd like to give him the finger.

With a bit more twisting and turning I manage to sink down into the chair.

I press the back of my hand to my upper lip and a damp smear rubs off. I have never experienced pain that is so bad it makes you properly sweat. Until now.

Shame it's impossible to transfer pain to someone else. At one time I'd have passed it on to Sergei in a heartbeat. But now he's here and trying his best to help me, I'm not so sure.

Dad parks up outside our flat.

'Hey, look who is there.' Sergei taps me on the shoulder and whispers from the back of the van where he and Angie are sitting uncomfortably. He nods to a figure that has just dodged behind a parked car. 'It is Linford.'

I keep watching as Linford emerges and crosses the street.

'Is that your mate?' Dad points, but I shrug and look the other way.

My face is burning when Dad insists on unfolding the wheelchair and we go through the same tortured palaver to get me into it.

I glance across the road and find, to my horror, that

Linford is standing there, watching us. His brow is furrowed and he digs his hands deeper into his pockets as I struggle to get in the chair. I expect him to laugh at my struggle or to shout something before running off, but if anything, he looks really worried.

'Just ignore him, Calum,' Sergei says in my ear.

A couple of younger kids who live at the end of the street lean back on a wall across the road and stare like it's free entertainment. They break eye-contact to whisper to each other and share a snigger.

As Linford walks past them, his head snaps up and he says something. The kids stop laughing and shuffle off without looking back.

'Are you feeling comfortable in your chair, Calum?' Sergei asks.

'Yeah, I'm fine, thanks.' I look back but Linford has disappeared. I bite the inside of my lip and look down at my lap. I thought he'd come to make fun of me but that doesn't seem to be the case.

Dad drapes his arm around Angie's shoulders and they watch as Sergei steps forward. He fusses around the wheelchair, checking the wheels are sturdy and the armrests steady, before grabbing the handles and steering me slowly towards the gate. He's being really helpful but I can't help thinking he's relishing the thought of being the one in charge.

'Let Dad do it,' I tell him. 'He'll be quicker than you.'

'I am managing fine. I am helping my friend,' he replies.

'Sergei is doing just fine there, Cal,' Dad remarks. 'Stop worrying.'

The logistics of getting into the flat prove to be another humiliating challenge.

The wheelchair is too wide for the front door, so I'm forced to get out and lean on Angie while Dad folds it up again. Sergei and Dad take an arm each and half drag, half carry me inside while my injured leg hangs uselessly like an overgrown puppet's.

'Do you need to visit the bathroom before you sit down?' Angie asks as we move past her.

'No,' I snap. As if I'd ask *her* to take me anyway.

The smile slides from her face and she steps away from me. I open my mouth to apologize, but then Dad and Sergei offload me into a comfortable chair and the moment passes.

Dad turns on the news and sits down to read the paper. I try to get on with reading *A Kestrel for a Knave*, but Sergei and Angie are busy in the kitchen, clattering pots and pans, and I find it hard to concentrate.

They are talking and laughing in Polish, most likely poking fun at my expense.

After a short time, their voices drop lower and I can hear urgent whispers between them. Whatever it is they're talking about sounds important. And secret.

I wish I could sneak over to the door and listen, see if they say anything in English, but I've no chance of moving from this chair on my own.

I feel my eyelids growing heavier, and after trying to fight it for a few minutes I eventually close my eyes, snapping awake twenty minutes later.

Dad is dozing on the settee, but half his newspaper has slid on to the floor and his mouth is lolling open. It's the sort of thing that would usually make me laugh. I might have even snapped a pic on my phone to tease him later. Today, it just makes my head ache more.

The most delicious smell permeates the flat. Despite having had no appetite in the hospital, my mouth begins to water. It is quieter now in the kitchen. The whispering has stopped and there is just the odd clink of cutlery, then Angie appears at the door with a tray, and coughs.

Dad wakes up with a start.

'Sorry . . .' He rubs his eyes and smooths back tufts of unruly hair. 'Must've dropped off.'

'Dinner is ready,' Angie announces grandly, walking towards me. 'I thought we would all eat in here so Calum is not dining alone.'

Me and Dad always eat on trays in front of the TV; you don't have much choice in a tiny flat like this. Angie talks as if there's a posh dining room with white tablecloths and solid-silver cutlery going spare somewhere down the hall. She places the tray down in front of me and I look down into the wide, flat dish that rests there.

The food smells amazing but it looks . . . gross.

I pick up the fork and poke at the dark brown mess. Seared chunks of lumpy meat nestle among something that looks like grey cabbage, tangled and unpleasant.

I lay the fork back down on the tray next to a hunk of weird-looking brown bread that looks as if it has been mixed with a load of grit before going in the oven.

'I made *bigos* for you,' Angie beams, undeterred.

Dad and Sergei have their trays now too and are already wolfing down the food.

'What's in it?'

'*Bigos* is a stew for hunters,' Sergei answers with his mouth full, although I wasn't talking to him. 'It is a Polish national dish.'

'Delicious,' Dad grunts, his head down.

'Yes, it is a – I think you would say here – a *hearty* stew made with kielbasa sausage, bacon and sauerkraut, among many more ingredients,' Angie explains, as if I'm actually interested. 'But here in Nottingham I find no kielbasa sausage, so I have to use only British sausage.'

I glance at the gritty bread.

'Oh, and I bake *razowy* bread for you also, of course.' She nods eagerly at the tray. 'It is a traditional Polish rye bread baked with many sorts of seeds.'

A few moments of silence pass while I wait for her to

go away again. I'll push the food around the dish a bit, make it look as if I've eaten some.

'Thank you, Angie,' Dad says, looking pointedly at me. 'We really appreciate you going to so much trouble.'

'Yeah, thanks,' I mumble, wishing I could just have a dish of instant noodles instead.

'Try it, Calum,' Sergei urges, breaking off another chunk of bread and dunking it into his stew.

Angie tries to smile at me but doesn't quite make it. She turns round and heads back to the kitchen slowly, like some of her sparkle just seeped away.

I look down at the tray again.

The food *does* smell delicious, and although it looks pretty weird, Angie has just confirmed there's nothing dodgy in it – like wild hedgehog or squirrels or whatever it is that I imagined Polish people might eat.

That, and the fact that I haven't eaten in a couple of days, decides it. I pick up the fork and spear a small piece of sausage. I eye the stringy stuff that has also found its way on to the fork.

'Sauerkraut.' Angie is back in the room and sitting down next to Dad with her tray of food. 'It is sort of a fermented, fine-cut cabbage.'

Fermented?

I'm about to put my fork down again when I catch one of Dad's legendary 'This Is Your First and Final Warning' looks.

Before I can overthink it any more, I slide the food into my mouth and chew.

I swallow, dig my fork in and take another, bigger mouthful. The moreish meat mixes with the sweetness of the sauerkraut and tomatoes.

It. Is. Delicious.

I watch everyone, even Dad, breaking bread and dipping it into the stew to soak up the gravy. I do the same. When I look up, Sergei is grinning.

'You like, yes, Calum?' he asks.

''S'all right,' I mumble, and Dad looks up sharply from his food. 'I mean, it's really nice – thanks, Angie.'

'You are most welcome, Calum.' She beams as if me liking her food somehow matters to her. 'How lovely we are sitting here in our new English home, eating Polish food together.'

She looks at Dad and they smile at each other.

I wonder if I'd ever have tried Polish food if it wasn't for Angie coming here. And the people who cook our Chinese takeaways and the posh Indian restaurant in town that me and Dad went to last year . . . would we have that choice if someone in the owners' families hadn't decided to come over here?

Calum grins at me and I take another big spoonful of *bigos* and smile back.

27

Monday. First proper day of the summer holidays.

I should be wolfing down my breakfast and then scooting down to the field to play footie all day with the lads. But of course, I'm not. I am more concerned with swallowing my painkillers on time.

I must have only had a couple of hours' kip last night. It feels like Sergei's mate Chopin is playing one of his Nocturnes up and down my leg – with a sledge-hammer.

'Dr Hall did say it would be tough for a few days,' Dad says, as if that makes it all OK. He pops the second pill out of its plastic bubble and hands it to me.

'Can't we get any stronger painkillers than this?' I swallow the second tablet down with a swig of tea. 'I can't stand this throbbing all day; it'll drive me nuts.'

'These are quite strong . . .' Dad inspects the label on the packet. 'You can only take them every four hours, too.'

Great. Every day, my life gets to be more of a train wreck.

'Let's get you into your chair.' Dad turns and calls out, 'Sergei!'

Seconds later, in Sergei bounces with that smug look pasted on to his face.

'Here I am, Pete.' He's all eager to please. The creep.

He drapes my other arm around his shoulders, and between them they manage to get me across the hall into the living room.

By the time I get my bum on the seat cushion, I'm dripping with perspiration and my leg feels like it's on fire.

'I'll pick your crutches up today,' Dad says, moving the table lamp next to me and placing my mug of tea next to it. 'Not as they'll be any use to you at the minute, but Dr Hall said, as soon as you feel up to it, you can start to move around a bit on them every day.'

I smirk as I think about the satisfaction I'd get from wrapping one of those crutches around Sergei's head when he's buzzing around me like a fly. Then I feel bad when I think about how he's trying to help me. I can't help wondering if I'd have been as caring if he'd been the one mowed down . . .

'That is better, Calum,' Sergei trills. 'Keep your neck up.'

Dad laughs. '*Chin* up, Sergei. It's *chin* up.'

'Ah, thank you, Pete. One day, I will get the hang of your strange British sayings.'

'Your English is brilliant, lad – isn't it, Calum?'

'Yeah.' I shrug. 'I suppose.'

*

Dad has got some local jobs on today, so he's not back home until later. It seems like he really did mean it at the hospital when he said he'd be spending more time at home.

When he's gone to work, Angie brings me in an omelette and a sliced tomato. For breakfast.

I look down at the food but I don't touch it.

'You must eat, Calum.' She plonks her hands on her hips.

'I don't want it.'

She never even asked what I fancied. Who eats anything but cereal for breakfast?

It wasn't that long ago, I could do what I liked. I made all the decisions in this flat when Dad was working away. Now I've got somebody else's mum acting like she's *my* mother, too.

'Come on. Just a few mouthfuls.'

'I. Don't. Want. It.' I don't look at her and she whisks the tray away.

'You know, you have got quite grumpy spending so much time alone,' she teases me. 'Luckily, you have us now, to keep you company.'

Angie goes to work and Sergei sidles back into the living room.

I don't know why, but I keep thinking about my mates. Linford, Jack and Harry – their faces shuffle in my mind like a pack of playing cards.

'I could build my next model in here, next to your chair?' Sergei offers. 'Perhaps you would like to watch how it is done.'

I grit my teeth as another flash of agony shoots from my hip, all the way down into my foot.

'Or perhaps we could—'

'Can't you just leave me alone?' I snap. 'I'm tired and I need these painkillers to start working. I can't even think straight with all this pain, never mind watch you play with building kits, like a big kid.'

'Of course.' Sergei walks backwards a few paces. 'You know, you are not the only one hurting, Calum. Do you ever think of anyone except yourself and how *you* are feeling?'

I close my eyes so I don't have to look at him, but his words echo in my ears like they want to be heard.

By mid-morning the sharpness of the pain has dulled slightly.

My legs don't feel like they're being pummelled and jabbed with knives any more, but now the constant dull throbbing is back and I'm starting to worry I might have to put up with it forever.

I decide to compose a text to send to Jack and Harry.

Got knocked over on estate on Fri. Can't walk, bored stiff. What you up to?

I delete the words 'bored stiff' as that makes me sound a bit sad.

Bad news spreads fast on the estate, so I know they'll have all heard about the hit-and-run. Dad showed me a paragraph in Saturday's *Nottingham Post*. It said the police were appealing for witnesses.

I purposely keep the text message simple, but hope they might be curious about what happened and want to know more. The two of them might come round later; they probably regret everything that's happened between us now.

I replace 'Can't walk' with 'Pins in leg'. Sounds more impressive. And painful.

It's best to let them know how serious it is. When bad stuff happens to people you care about, it makes you realize what's important.

Got knocked over on estate on Fri. Pins in leg. What you up to?

I fire off the text and wait.

And wait.

I stare at my phone on the arm of the chair.

The screen remains blank and unlit. Nobody replies.

28

Sergei brings through his battered suitcase full of cardboard. He's trying hard to entertain me, and although I find him irritating, I am also mildly curious.

'I'm sorry,' I say, before I can think better of it. 'For snapping at you earlier, I mean.'

'It is OK, Calum, I did not notice.' He looks at me. 'After a while, you get used to it. Being an outsider, I mean.'

I don't know what to say to that.

Sergei opens the suitcase on the floor next to me. He lifts pieces out and holds them up to the light, glancing at me to see if I'm still watching. I wonder how he creates those lifelike structures from something that looks so shabby and flat.

'What do you think my next project should be, Calum?' he says, even though I've got my eyes closed now, feigning sleep. 'The Burj Khalifa or the Eiffel Tower?'

'I don't know.' I open my eyes. 'You choose.'

'Yes, I think I shall.' He smiles to himself. 'I shall build what I want to build.'

He picks out several pieces of card and lays them

aside, closing the suitcase again.

I close my eyes again, but every so often I open them so slightly it still appears as if I'm asleep.

An hour later, Sergei is still building.

He slots together the pieces of cardboard, making sure the base is sturdy and balanced before continuing.

I watch him through eyes narrowed into slits. His tongue sticks out and his brow is furrowed as he stares intently at the plan, his fingers working deftly to create something, to fit the pieces of the puzzle together.

I think he's forgotten I'm here. I think he's forgotten everything apart from the task in hand. It's the way I feel when I put together a screenplay: the outside world ceases to exist in my mind.

Two hours later I open my eyes and realize I actually have fallen asleep for a while. Sergei is no longer in the room.

I take in a sharp breath. There, right in front of me, is a towering black structure, glittering with tiny lights.

The Burj Khalifa.

If I was standing upright, the tip of the model would reach up to my shoulders.

'The real thing is two thousand, seven hundred and seventeen feet tall.' Sergei walks in carrying two plates stacked with sandwiches and crisps. 'Twice as tall as the

Empire State Building, and three times the height of the Eiffel Tower.'

'Where did you get the fancy lights?' I wonder aloud.

'Oh, it is just one light inside the structure, see?' He pulls out a cardboard compartment at the bottom where a small bulb is fitted. 'It came with the kit. Two batteries run all of the lights. An optical illusion.'

They look like individual tiny lights, but close up I can see now that the whole structure is peppered with tiny round holes that let the light shine through.

'Clever,' I murmur.

My stomach growls at the sight of the food. Sergei puts one of the plates down on the arm of my chair.

I pick up a sandwich. 'Thanks for making this.'

'You are welcome, Calum. So, tell me, what do you think to my masterpiece?'

''S'all right,' I say with my mouth full.

'The Burj Khalifa has the most floors of any building on the planet,' he continues, looking at the model in awe. 'Did you know its design was inspired by a desert flower named *Hymenocallis* that has long petals extending down from its centre?'

'No,' I say. 'I didn't. How come you know all this stuff, anyway?'

'I am interested in the subject. Therefore, I find out the most interesting facts.'

Oh yeah, I forgot what a smart alec he can be.

'You know lots of information about films, yes? This is because you are interested in them.'

'I suppose so. But I don't know how you can be bothered spending hours building this stuff.' I cram a handful of crisps into my mouth. 'Your Burj Khalifa looks great, but what's the point, really? I mean, what you gonna actually *do* with it?'

'I will put it on my shelf,' he states simply.

'Yes, but I mean, what's it for?'

Still seems like a waste of time to me.

'I don't build the structures *for* any purpose,' Sergei continues. 'It is the process of getting there which I enjoy. That is what brings the real satisfaction.'

It sounds like a good way to write my screenplay. I resolve to concentrate on the process rather than the outcome. To work methodically through from the basic structure to the fancy pieces.

Then it won't matter that I could never win the competition.

After lunch I have to suffer the embarrassment of Sergei helping me to the loo.

'Thanks,' I mutter when I finally sink back down into the chair. The thudding in my leg is getting worse and Sergei fetches me more painkillers and a glass of water.

'Is there anything else I can get for you?'

I almost feel bad for being so moody with him. I'm

about to say no when I remember.

'My rucksack, please. It's at the end of my bed.'

He brings it in and puts it next to my chair.

'Calum, I have to go out,' he says, 'but it will not be for long. Will you be OK?'

'Course I'll be OK,' I say. 'I'm not a complete cripple, you know.'

Sergei looks at my useless leg but doesn't say anything.

'I'll be fine,' I say. 'Just go.'

When I hear the back door close I pick up my phone again. There are still no replies to my text from the lads.

I hear a noise – a sort of shuffle – and then a bang outside. I put my phone back down on the arm of the chair and sit very still, listening. Maybe Sergei has forgotten something and come back.

But he doesn't return.

Sergei has left the back door unlocked and I can barely move. If someone wanted to come in and steal from us or attack me, there's nothing I could do about it. I should have told him to lock it on his way out.

I think about the other night and Linford's furious expression when he stood outside, looking up at the window. Stories I've heard about gangs on the estate using baseball bats on people when they've got a grudge against someone . . . I think about that, too.

Then a door slams shut downstairs and all is quiet again. It's probably just Mr Baxter taking out his rubbish. I smile at my own overactive imagination. I've got too much time on my hands and not enough to do.

I reach down and grab my rucksack. I plunge my hand in and feel around a bit until my fingers close on the notebook Freya gave me.

I turn to a clean page and pick up a pen.

I've got my idea and I'm going to build the structure with my words.

Since I put the outcome of the competition out of my mind, I feel free to just write what I want to without worrying whether or not the judges will like it, or if it holds up to the standard of the other entrants.

It doesn't matter any more because, to adapt Sergei's earlier phrase, 'I shall write what I want to write.'

Sergei is gone for nearly three hours.

When he gets back, he pops his head in the door.

I tell him no thanks, I don't want anything.

'Where did you get to?' I ask.

He mumbles something incoherent and disappears into my bedroom. He doesn't come back come until Dad gets back at about four o'clock.

'What you up to, son?' Dad asks as I scribble away.

'Just working on an idea I have for a screenplay,' I say. 'It's just something I feel like doing.'

'Good for you,' Dad says, but I can see he looks a bit baffled.

Dad makes three mugs of strong tea and shouts Sergei through to join us. I wish he hadn't. I can't remember the last time we had any time on our own, just me and Dad.

'I've got a few local jobs on this week, so I'll be nearby if you need me,' Dad says. 'In fact I've got to pop out again after tea. There's been more vandalism at the Expressions centre this afternoon. They've asked me to pop by and have a look what's what.'

My ears prick up and I put down my pen.

'Have they caught who's doing it?' I ask Dad. 'The vandalism.'

'No, but it must've happened in broad daylight this afternoon, as everything was apparently OK when Shaz locked up after lunch.' Dad says. 'She told me if they don't catch the culprit, they're in danger of losing their funding, and if that happens, they might even have to close down. Anyway, I'll go and have a look at the damage.'

I look up to see Sergei standing in the doorway, listening.

'Can I come with you?' I say to Dad. 'I haven't been out of the house in my wheelchair yet.'

Dad looks at me.

'I'm going to find it hard enough going back there, son,' Dad says tightly. 'Those – those *cowards* mowed you down in cold blood right outside the centre. It might bring it all back for you.'

I look at Dad's hands, clenching and unclenching.

'It might,' I try to reason. 'But Expressions is on our doorstep. It's not as if I can avoid it forever.'

'I know that.' He sighs and rubs his forehead. 'But it might be a bit soon. Once they've caught whoever did it, you might feel a bit safer. That's all.'

'I'll feel safe if I'm with you.'

Dad shrugs. 'Fine, then,' he says. 'If you really want to. Do you fancy tagging along, Sergei?'

'No. No, thank you,' Sergei says quickly and takes a step back. 'I have some homework I must do, but thank you for asking, Pete.'

'He's been out all afternoon, Dad,' I say. 'Haven't you, Sergei?'

'Yes. I had some things to do for Mama. I will see you both later,' he says, disappearing into my bedroom.

I'm perplexed why Sergei seems to have scuttled off so quickly when Dad mentioned going to the centre, but all thoughts of that disappear when I start to think about the accident. I don't mention it to Dad, but I'm hoping it might jog my memory when I see the spot where it happened again.

The police don't seem to have any leads yet, but surely someone's got to know *something*. I can't sleep or do anything at all without the pain intruding. Why should the culprits get away with that?

And someone has been vandalizing the centre. What if

that's somehow linked to the accident?

A flash of a memory, a voice, flits through my mind, but it's gone as soon as it appears.

I look up to see Sergei in the doorway again, tapping his foot on the floor and watching me.

Finally Dad gets me out of the flat and into my wheelchair. Sergei helps but disappears again when we're ready to leave.

'I could've been there and back by now,' Dad complains.

'Yeah, well, I'm sorry to put you out, but you're not stuck in the flat day in, day out, are you?' I frown. 'You don't know what it's like.'

'I know, lad, but it won't be for long.'

No, just the whole flipping summer.

Something in my chest fizzes when I think what's happened and how the person who drove into me is out there, living their life as normal. I grip the arms of the wheelchair, digging my fingertips deep into the shiny cushioned plastic.

Dad pushes me down the street, whistling.

'I was wondering,' I say. 'What if whoever is vandalizing the centre knows something about who knocked me over?'

'What makes you think that?' Dad replies.

'It's just a thought,' I say with a shrug. 'But can you mention it to PC Bolton?'

Dad stops walking and comes round the front of my wheelchair.

'Is anything coming back to you, son?' Dad crouches down and studies my face. 'Anything . . . anything at all we can tell the police might help. Even if you think it's not—'

'Dad.' I sigh. 'Chill out. I'm just suggesting something that might help.'

'I know, but it's driving me crazy.' Dad thumps the arm of the chair as he stands up and it makes me jump. 'Sorry, I'm really sorry, Calum. It's just . . . the thought that the culprit is out there, laughing at us. I can't stand it.'

Dad's face looks lined and tired.

'I know,' I say quietly. 'I know.'

'This is Shazia Khan, the centre manager.' Dad introduces me to a short, plump woman with a big smile but an anxious face. I realize she's the woman I saw unlocking the centre gates before the recent meeting about the screenplay. 'Shaz, this is my son, Calum.'

'Please, call me Shaz. Your dad told me about the hit-and-run, Calum. It's a terrible business and we're speaking to the police about making it safer outside our gates.' She holds out her hand and I shake it. 'I think I've seen you down here before, haven't I?'

'I came to the meeting here,' I say. 'About the screenwriting.'

Dad looks at me as if I'm speaking in Japanese or something.

'Ah yes, the competition.' Shaz beams. 'You going to have a go?'

'Dunno . . .' I shrug.

'Looks like it could be the ideal project for you while you're recovering from the accident,' Shaz says, and then turns her attention to Dad. 'If you can secure the windows please, Pete, then just take a look around to see if there are any obvious weaknesses in the security.'

'You got CCTV here?' Dad looks around the foyer.

Shaz frowns and shakes her head. 'I'm afraid our funding doesn't stretch to that. We have a big bid currently being considered, and if we're successful we'll be improving our security system right away.' Her face lights up talking about the possibility, but then her eyes fade dull. 'They're coming to assess us in two weeks' time but we're up against some of the best facilities in the region. If the centre is wrecked from vandalism and break-ins when they visit us, that's our chances gone, I'm afraid.'

'It's probably just kids off school with nothing to do,' Dad says, frowning.

'Only, the police have said this isn't just bored local kids. And it's been happening for weeks.' Shaz's face drops. 'They reckon we're talking organized, wilful damage here.'

'What makes them think that?'

'Well, whoever it is seems to be targeting certain areas, destroying key IT and sound equipment that makes it increasingly difficult to continue our work.' Shaz sighs. 'The scary thing is, there's been no sign of forced entry, so we don't even know how they're getting in. The only explanation is that it's someone with a key.'

Before I can think better of it, I interrupt their conversation.

'Shaz, I know this sounds mad . . .' I say. They both turn to look at me. 'But I think I might have an idea how they are getting in.'

'Here he is, our hero,' Dad announces when we get to the flat. He helps me up the stairs and then sits me back down in my wheelchair.

Angie is back home and she walks into the hallway, smiling.

'Our Calum's only just gone and solved the mystery of the local community centre's vandalism,' he says proudly. 'He found something even the police managed to miss.'

My bedroom door opens and Sergei leans sulkily against the wall to listen.

I tell Angie how I'd seen someone lurking around at the side of the centre, near the bins.

'So, when me and Shaz go and check –' Dad takes over

224

the story – 'what do we find? Tucked behind the biggest, heaviest bin at the back is a small concealed hatch to the basement. Looks like a workman might have left it unlocked by mistake at some point.'

'That's how they've been getting in,' I chip in.

'Brilliant, well done, Calum!' Angie beams.

Dad pats me on the head like a well-behaved dog and while they fuss around the flat getting stuff moved out of the way so someone can push me through into the sitting room, Sergei sidles over to me.

'Bravo, Calum,' he says with a faint smile. 'It seems you are quite the detective.'

He's pretending to be impressed but I can tell he isn't really.

Suddenly I remember how, on the afternoon of the accident, I was supposed to be meeting him at the school gates to walk home together. But, of course, he didn't turn up.

Lucky for him. He would have been with me when the speeding car appeared from nowhere.

I can't help wondering where Sergei got to. Where was he, while I was under the wheels of that car?

I look up to ask him, just in time to see the bedroom door closing.

Dad goes to the chippy for tea, so we get normal food instead of Polish stuff.

After we've all scoffed our fish and chips, Dad clears his throat.

'Right, we've got something to tell you both,' he says. 'Angie?'

Angie looks down at her hands, and Sergei and I look at each other.

'I have to go back to Poland,' she says in a small voice. 'My papa, he is sick and needs—'

'Dziadek is ill?' Sergei jumps up. He pronounces it *Jah-dek*. It sounds like one of the strange words he was saying in his sleep. 'Mama, I will come with you.'

He rushes over to sit next to Angie.

'No, Sergei, I cannot take you with me this time. Dziadek is in the hospital and there is much to be done, tests that must be carried out. Perhaps when he is better, you can—'

'No! I must come with you.'

Angie throws up her hands and looks at Dad, exasperated.

'Come on, Sergei, lad. Listen to your mum, she knows what's best for you.'

Sergei glares at Dad, and then at his mum, and storms out of the room, knocking over Angie's glass of wine on the way and slamming the door behind him.

Dad's jaw drops open and I feel a little twist of satisfaction that finally he's glimpsed a side of Sergei that only I seem to have seen up until now.

226

If Sergei has a hidden side, maybe Angie does too. I mean, how well can Dad really know her after such a short time? Things seemed to escalate very fast between them. Met at work one minute . . . moving in the next.

Dad's no fool, but I know part of him is lonely, after Mum.

And there are people in this world that know just how to exploit a situation like that.

Angie and Dad both go to the bedroom to try and speak to Sergei. Angie comes out crying ten minutes later and shuts herself in Dad's bedroom.

'He just keeps pulling the quilt over his head; he won't even look at us,' Dad tells me when he comes back into the living room. 'Can you go and see if you can get through to him, Calum?'

'Me? And say what?'

'You'll think of something. It's hard for him, you know,' Dad says, as if this is somehow my fault. 'While Angie's away for a few days, I've got a fairly clear diary, so the good news is the three of us can do some man-stuff together. And I'll be home for your birthday on Thursday.'

The *three* of us? Great.

At least he's remembered it's my birthday later in the week, though, which makes a change.

*

227

Dad helps me hobble through to the bedroom on my crutches. They feel bulky and sore under my armpits, pressing on to my bruised flesh. I wouldn't be able to tolerate using them for more than a few steps. Dad sits me down on the end of my bed. Then he walks out without saying another word and closes the door behind him.

I can see the outline of Sergei under his quilt, but he's covered himself up completely; there's just a single tuft of hair visible on his pillow.

The throbbing in my legs is so bad I can't even try to speak to Sergei. I close my eyes and wait for it to pass.

All I can do is concentrate on my breathing until the pain abates a little. I feel sick and hot, and I am frightened to move a muscle in case it makes it even worse.

I look across at Sergei's shelf. The Burj Khalifa sits next to the Empire State Building. The twinkly lights aren't on now, but it is still impressive.

I think about the notes I've started to make on my screenplay. I've got my main idea down now and I'm thinking about the characters.

After a few minutes, Sergei pulls the quilt down a bit and peers out at me.

'Are you OK, Calum? Your face looks very pale.'

'Yeah? Well you'd probably pass out if you had pain like this.'

Then I remember I'm supposed to be trying to be a bit nicer to him.

'I do understand because I have pain right now,' he says softly. 'Heart pain can also be unbearable.'

I don't know what to say.

'You saw the picture of Dziadek when we were at school, yes?'

'Yeah,' I say with a shrug, remembering the photograph in his rucksack that Linford crumpled and tossed aside.

'He was a young man in that picture. Strong, and the head of the Zurakowski family. Dziadek has always been there for me, Calum, as long as I can remember.'

I think about Grandad, how he was around when I was happy, always there when I felt sad or worried. I could talk to him about anything; somehow we just understood each other.

'It is my turn to be there for Dziadek, now *he* is in need, you know?'

I do know.

Grandad's breathing failed him in the end; the coroner wrote 'chronic bronchitis with breathing complication'. He was ill for weeks beforehand and he fought like a soldier before it finally got the better of him.

I used to call in on him on my way to school and every night, too, on my way home. Between us, me and Dad looked after him, and with his daily home-help visit, it meant he could stay in his own home until the end. That was really important to Grandad, to stay in the place he felt safe. Old people don't like change; they like to sit among their memories.

'Decades of fun and laughter are trapped in these very walls,' Grandad used to say. 'I can still hear your gran's voice when I listen hard.'

Gran and Grandad had lived in that house all their married life. Even though it was too big for him when Gran died, Grandad said he'd never move. And he didn't. He took his last breath at home in the very bedroom where my dad was born.

'I understand,' I say quietly to Sergei.

'You do?'

'I have got feelings, you know,' I say.

'Yes, I can see this now.' Sergei nods. 'But you have kept them very well hidden up until this moment, Calum.'

The cheeky so-and-so.

'I want to go home with Mama, to show Dziadek I am still here for him. She should not stop me.'

'I'd feel the same as you, Sergei, honestly I would,' I say. 'But he sounds a proud man, your old fella. He might not want you to see him feeling so unwell. Maybe it's best he gets the medical help he needs first and then you can go back when he's feeling stronger.'

Sergei frowns as he considers this.

'Perhaps you are correct after all, Calum,' he says, staring into space. 'If only we had not come over to England, I would not have this problem. I would be by

Dziadek's bedside this very moment.'

'That's true,' I agree.

I can't help thinking that they should've thought about that before they rushed over here, but for once I decide to keep my mouth shut.

'I told Mama that I did not want to leave Warsaw. I did not want to travel 928 miles to this place.'

'You mean you didn't want to come here?' I'd always believed the headlines I'd seen on Dad's newspaper; that Eastern European people were all clamouring to come here. And the stuff Linford was always repeating. 'So why did your mum still make you come?'

'It became dangerous at home.' Sergei shrugged. 'My father, he is a violent man. He hurt Mama. He hurt me. He hurt our pet animals, too. Mama left him once before, but he found us again and he broke her arm.'

'Did you go to the police?'

'Yes, the police had an arrest warrant out for him, but when you are afraid, it is not easy to believe people can help. Even the police.'

'What did you do?'

'We ran, started again in a new place, but every night we were too afraid to sleep. Mama gave him one more chance, but it happened again. That's when she said we had to come to England.'

The back of my neck prickles as he describes their life. I had no idea.

231

'But I thought you just wanted . . .'

I press my lips together tightly. I've said too much already.

'Benefits, housing, *a free ride*, as your friend Linford likes to say? This is really what you think we want above our home, our family?'

I look down at the floor.

We both stay silent for a few moments.

'I wish with all my heart I was back there,' Sergei says, his voice flat and empty. 'Home.'

His eyes look dark and shiny. I'm not sure what I should say to make him feel better. I think about the assumptions I've made and I hang my head.

'You'd still go back?' I remark.

'Yes, I would still go back, even though both Mama and I were so afraid there. I did not want to leave my beloved Warsaw. I did not want to leave my best friend Pawel, or my rabbits and my dog. I did not want to leave our little house on the edge of the wood where the squirrels come to the windowsills each morning to eat breakfast.'

A tear rolls down the side of his face and leaves a clean, wet track. I look away.

'Most of all, I did not want to leave Dziadek.'

He throws off the quilt at last and sits up on his bed.

'It sounds like you're better off here, mate,' I say. 'At least until it's safe.'

Sergei bites his lip as if he's trying to find the right words.

'But my home is in here.' He taps his chest. 'It stays there, even when you move away or have bad times. It is a place that you want to return to someday.'

I think about Amelia and Sergei. Their home is a place they love; for me, home is somewhere I can't wait to escape from.

★

EXT. SUMMERTIME - KABATY, WARSAW - DAY
Small, single-storey detached house stands at edge of a wood. Two windows and a door with a red tiled roof. There are other similar houses dotted here and there further along the edge of the wood.

A line of washing sways slightly in the warm breeze. Birdsong. The sound of the odd car from the road behind the wood. The sound of a WOMAN singing drifts through the window now and then. Otherwise, it is quiet.

BOY ONE sits in full sun on a patch of grass in front of the house with BOY TWO, his best friend. They are building a structure.

                    BOY TWO
            Hey, it is my turn now!

                    BOY ONE
      In a moment, my friend. Have patience.
      Remember, I am the master builder!

A long-legged black dog runs by and knocks
over part of the building the boy is working
on.

                    BOY ONE
    Hey, Baron! Bad dog! I'll thank you to stay
              away from my masterpiece.

The dog turns and yaps, wagging his tail.

BOY TWO shakes his head and rolls his eyes,
and both boys laugh.

                    BOY ONE
      That is one crazy dog, but he is like my
    brother. My dog brother and best friend. As
              you are my best friend.

BOY TWO nods and smiles, picks up a
small stick and throws it. The dog barks

                      234

and chases after it.

> BOY TWO
>
> You are my best friend, too.

> BOY ONE
>
> (*grins*)
>
> I know this trick. Some people will say anything for a turn to build, yes?

> BOY TWO
>
> (*calls, taunting*)
>
> That's right! But what are you going to do about it?

BOY TWO jumps up laughing and runs to edge of wood.

BOY ONE laughs and jumps up, begins to run towards his friend. The boys yell, chasing each other in and out of the trees.

A rumble of an engine stops both boys in their tracks. They fall silent and look at each other. BOY ONE's face drains of colour.

They dash behind a nearby tree and watch as

a burly MAN in a checked shirt and jeans
jumps down from a jeep-style vehicle. There
are freshly cut tree trunks in the open boot
of the vehicle.

The dog runs to greet MAN as he jumps from
the jeep. MAN kicks out and the dog yelps
and limps away.

MAN stands and glares at BOY ONE's building
project on the front lawn. His face is red
and sweaty. He is scowling. He takes a long
drink from the can of beer he clutches in
one meaty hand.

MAN

(*throws back head and yells*)

What is this crap doing out here, left for
someone else to tidy up again? Where is the
boy?

WOMAN comes rushing out of house, wiping her
hands on a towel.

WOMAN

(*nervously*)

Oh! You are home so early!

MAN

(*face darkens*)

So, a man can't return to his own house when
he pleases? A fine welcome. Where is the
boy?

The WOMAN's eyes dart over to the woods. She
turns back to the MAN and smiles nervously.

WOMAN

I am so pleased to see you are home early!
Come in, *Bejbe*. I have a cold lemonade and I
just this minute took cakes from the oven.

MAN

(*yells*)

Are you deaf, woman? *Where is that good-for-
nothing boy?*

He takes a final swig of beer and tosses the
can into the bushes.

WOMAN

(*close to tears*)

H-he is with his friend, *Bejbe*. I think they
went for a walk. Please don't—

                    MAN
               (*clenches fists*)
Please don't what? Don't teach him a lesson?
Maybe I should teach you the lesson instead,
                     huh?

He lumbers towards the WOMAN. She squeezes
her eyes shut but doesn't move.

BOY ONE steps forward from the trees.

                  BOY ONE
            (*quietly, head down*)
               Here I am, Papa.

The MAN stops walking towards the WOMAN and
turns to the BOY.

                    MAN
Oh, you are ready to face me like a man now!
 Instead of running around the woods like a
      baby with your . . . little friend.

BOY TWO whispers something to BOY ONE and
slopes away into the woods.

MAN nods to the structure outside the house.

                     238

                    MAN
You left a mess for your mother to clean up.

                   BOY ONE
   The building is not yet finished, Papa. I
                   was just—

                    MAN
                  (*slurring*)
              You left a mess.

                   BOY ONE
   I am sorry, Papa. I will clean it up right
                    now.

As BOY ONE walks by him, MAN lashes out and
catches him on the side of the head. BOY ONE
loses his balance and falls over.

                   WOMAN
                  (*crying*)
              You hurt him!

She runs to help her son. MAN storms towards
them both.

CUT TO:

The trees swaying gently in the breeze. Different shapes and shades of green leaves against the blue sky.

Sounds of hurting. A slap. A thud. A boy cries out. A woman screams.
Birds scatter, a squirrel runs up a tree.

Then the sound of a car door slamming. An engine revving.

CUT TO:

The MAN jumps back into his vehicle and drives away. Dust flies up from the dirt road. Then, silence.

CUT TO:

BOY ONE and his mother sit holding each other on the grass. WOMAN's nose is bleeding. The dog limps up to them and nuzzles BOY ONE's face.

WOMAN

(*crying*)

This time we must leave, my son. Right now, before he gets back.

BOY ONE

(*alarmed, stroking the dog's head*)

But . . . what about my friend? What about
Baron and Dziadek? Surely, we cannot leave
again, Mama.

WOMAN

(*stares into space*)

We have no choice. We will take Baron to
Dziadek's house and then we must get away
from here.

BOY ONE

Where will we go?

WOMAN

To England, where we always planned to go.
And one day, I promise you, Sergei, we will
return here. One day, we will come back home.

END SCENE.

241

29

The next day, when we wake up, Angie's flights have already been booked online and Dad is up and dressed, ready to drive her to East Midlands Airport.

I stay in my bedroom while Sergei says goodbye to his mum. When he comes back in, his eyes are red and he keeps sniffing like he has a cold.

I've had Sergei's screenplay swirling round in my head all night. It's left a sour taste at the back of my throat, as if while I'm sleeping I've been trying to swallow down all the mean things I've said and all the stuff I've watched being done to him since he arrived in England.

I'd like to take it all back, now I know the truth, but I don't know how to.

Angie puts her head around the door before she leaves.

'Goodbye, Calum. Soon, I will be back.'

'Bye, Angie, have a safe journey,' I say, and I mean it. After Sergei confided in me, I think about how she might not be safe.

When they've gone, Sergei helps me get dressed, and eventually we manage to get into the sitting room.

*

Two hours later, Dad strolls back in with doughnuts and vanilla milkshakes from McDonald's.

'Thank you, Pete. This is a good treat.' Sergei brings some plates through. His eyes look far away but I can see he's trying to be brave about his grandad.

'I rang the coppers like you asked me, Calum,' Dad says, handing me a doughnut. 'Spoke to PC Channer. He made a note but doesn't think it's very likely there's any connection between the break-ins at the centre and your accident.'

A stab of annoyance jabs at my chest. 'How does he know? If he hasn't found who's thieving from the centre, he can't know for sure.'

Dad doesn't answer. I feel a burning urge to go out there and knock on doors to ask questions. Anything but sitting here, completely useless and reliant on others.

I watch Dad carefully as he hands me the paper cup with a straw. He's avoiding my eyes, for some reason.

I've seen him like this before and I recognize the signs. He's got something to say that he's not looking forward to telling me.

'So, what "man-stuff" have you got planned for us today then, Dad?' I nudge him.

Sergei looks up from tearing his doughnut into bite-size pieces. 'Man-stuff?'

'Yeah, Dad's cleared his diary to spend more time with us while your mum's away.' I wipe a smear of jam from

243

my chin with the back of my hand.

'This is good news, Pete.' Sergei seems to cheer up a bit. 'Perhaps we can go to the bowling alley?'

'Well, that was the plan, of course, but . . .' Dad stammers. His eyes dart around the room while he thinks of the best way to drop the bombshell I can feel is coming. 'But it won't be today or tomorrow, I'm afraid.'

'Today *or* tomorrow?'

He can't be serious. I really thought he'd changed.

'I got a call driving back from the airport,' he explains. 'This gem of a job has come up, Calum; it could seriously set us up. I swear this will be the last time – one last job.'

'Until the next "gem of a job" comes up, that is,' I snap. 'I believed you, Dad. When you said you'd stay home because of me, I was stupid enough to swallow it.'

'I meant every word of it, son.' His face drops. If I didn't know better, I might think he was genuinely feeling bad about it. 'I don't need to do the dodgy jobs now for money like before. Me and Angie are sharing the bills now, and things are much easier. I'm only going to be taking work on that's above board. No more dodgy stuff.'

'Then why are you doing *this* job?'

'I'd already agreed to it – and besides, it'll help us get our heads above water once and for all. Just means me driving to France for a couple of—'

'*France?*' For as long as I can remember, Dad's next job

is always going to 'set us up'. Of course, it never turns out to be as lucrative as he's hoping.

'It's just some stuff that needs to be collected and brought back to the UK,' Dad says, as if he's just going down the road and I shouldn't be making such a big deal about it.

'Not drugs, I hope, Pete?' Sergei says, his face lined with concern.

I want to laugh but I'm annoyed with Dad and I don't want to let him think he can squirm out of a proper excuse.

'Give me some credit, Sergei.' Dad frowns. 'Not drugs, no.'

'What then?' I demand. I'm sick of Dad's bluffing and half-answers. He's my dad. I should know how he earns money. He's already admitted it's dodgy; he might as well spill the beans.

'Designer handbags, if you must know,' Dad replies.

If anyone asks, just tell them I'm in imports and exports, I remember Dad saying.

Then it hits me.

'Dad, are these handbags counterfeit?'

Dad looks up sharply from eating his doughnut.

'What does this word mean?' Sergei asks. '*Counter-feit*?'

'It means *fake*,' I say, looking at Dad. 'And fake designer handbags aren't just dodgy, they're illegal.'

'I've been stupid, I know that, but I don't need *you* telling me what to do.' Dad stands up, his face red and his jaw clenched. 'This is the last one. I mean it this time.'

He throws a twenty-pound note on the table before stuffing his wallet in the back pocket of his jeans and walking out of the room.

I hear his bedroom door open and then he's rifling around in the wardrobe. The familiar sounds of Dad packing a bag filter through to the living room. My heart sinks.

A few minutes later he's in the doorway.

'I'm off now, back tomorrow evening. Don't do anything I wouldn't do, eh?' He walks a few steps to leave, and then turns back when Sergei calls his name.

'What about Calum? I mean, what if he needs to go to hospital again?' He looks fearfully at my leg. 'I will have to call Mama if there is an emergency—'

'No need to tell your mum about this, Sergei. I don't want her worrying about you two, on top of everything else. She's got enough on her plate.' Dad gives me the thumbs-up. 'Calum will be fine – won't you, lad?'

'Doesn't sound as if I've got much choice,' I say with a scowl.

Dad winks at us from the door, his bad mood already forgotten. He raises his hand and then he's gone.

Sergei looks at me, confused. 'Mama has a plate?'

I shake my head. 'It's just a way of saying your mum

has a lot of worries on her mind at the moment.'

'I see,' he says. 'This British way of speaking can be complicated.'

I can't argue with that.

I listen as the back door slams, and a few minutes later Dad's diesel van coughs into life.

Sergei is chewing noisily with his mouth open – 'clapping', Grandad used to call it. I put my own doughnut down and stare at the wall.

Two full days with nothing to do apart from listen to Sergei eating noisily, and it's still only the first week of the summer holidays.

Somebody kill me now.

The next afternoon, I'm reading *A Kestrel for a Knave* when my phone buzzes with a text.

I snatch it up, thinking it might be one of the lads finally getting in touch.

Will ring in 5 mins. Dad.

I've got a bad feeling about this. Dad hardly ever calls me when he's away unless he's going to be delayed on a job. And it's my birthday tomorrow.

I answer on the first ring.

'I'm sorry, lad, but I'm stuck on this job. Any luck, I should be back Thursday evening.'

'OK.' I can hear the disappointment in my own voice, but I should be used to it by now.

'We'll celebrate your birthday at the weekend, I promise.' Dad is speaking too fast, like he can't wait to get off the phone. 'We've got some big problems here and I can't get—'

'Dad, it's fine.' I sigh. I've heard all his excuses before. 'See you when you get back.'

'Good lad.' Dad sounds relieved. 'Tell Sergei again he needs to keep shtum about this. No need for Angie to be worrying while she's away.'

Dad ends the call and I sit for a few moments staring at my phone.

Sergei comes through with two glasses of milk.

'It will be fine,' Sergei says when I tell him about Dad's call. He takes a long slurp of his milk, leaving a ring of froth around his mouth. 'We will survive, Calum.'

'It's not *your* birthday that's going to be cancelled,' I point out, feeling miffed.

'No birthdays will be cancelled while I am in charge,' Sergei says firmly.

I scowl at him. 'Who said *you* were in charge?'

We stare each other out for a few seconds and then, for no reason at all, we both burst out laughing.

30

The next morning, I wake up and look across to Sergei's bed to find it empty. I can hear him banging around in the kitchen.

I can't get out of bed on my own, so I'll just have to wait until he reappears. My legs are banging with pain. The bottom of my back is damp and my stomach feels a bit queasy, probably with the pain medication.

Five minutes later, the door opens and Sergei makes his way back into the bedroom, carrying a tray weighed down with food and drinks.

He lowers the tray slowly down on to his camp bed. I breathe in a sweet, delicious aroma, but all I really want is for the pain to go away.

'*Wszystkiego najlepszego z okazji urodzin*, Calum!'

'Eh?'

'It means *All the best on your birthday*!' Sergei beams and hands me a glass of fresh orange juice and, even better, two painkillers.

'Oh right, yeah. Ta.' I swallow the tablets.

He offers me a dish of fruit: apples and oranges cut up into little segments. I don't know what it is about Polish people, but they never seem to just eat Weetabix for breakfast.

I take a bit of apple but I don't eat it.

'For your birthday treat, I bake for you a very sweet cake.' He picks up a plate and hands it to me.

It smells good, so I take a bite and chew. It is still warm and tastes delicious.

'You like my Polish fried cherry cake?'

I swallow down another mouthful of cake and nod. 'Very nice, thanks.'

He hands me a card. On the front is a picture of a teddy bear. It might be a suitable card if I was turning five years old today.

He watches me.

'Sorry, it was all the shop had.'

'Thanks, it's great,' I say, smiling. 'It's the thought that counts.'

'Oh, and I got you this.'

He hands me a grubby paperback book. I read the title: *The Loneliness of the Long-Distance Runner*. I've never heard of it.

'Thanks,' I say.

'It is a story about a troubled boy who copes with his problems by focusing on his love for running. I see you have nearly finished your other book so I thought you could read this one next.'

I want to choose my next read myself, maybe with Mr

Ahmed's help. But it's nice of Sergei to try and pick one as a gift.

'Sounds great, thanks,' I say politely.

'It was written by a man called Alan Sillitoe,' Sergei says, beaming. 'A fellow Nottinghamian just like you, Calum, who wrote about the lives of working-class people.'

'Eh?' I look at the cover again.

'The book was made into a film and Mr Sillitoe wrote the screenplay, too.'

Alan Sillitoe . . . I say the name in my head: a real writer, who was born in Nottingham? I turn to the inside page and my eyes widen.

'Says here his father worked at the Raleigh Bicycle Company and Alan worked there when he first left school,' I say as I scan the short author biography. 'That's where my grandad, George Brooks, worked all his life.'

'Exactly, Calum.' Sergei looks pleased with himself. 'So you see, you already have a good start, just like Alan Sillitoe, for writing your screenplay.'

I can't believe it. All the stories my grandad told me about working at Raleigh – like when a man lost his hand because everyone stood around in shock . . . Then I get to thinking: maybe he even *knew* Alan Sillitoe before he became a famous writer . . .

★

**INT. RALEIGH BICYCLE FACTORY, NOTTINGHAM –
1944 – AFTERNOON**

The Pedal and Bar factory floor is large and
dusty. Machinery is clunking and clicking,
the workers are chattering; somewhere a
radio plays. Bicycle parts can be identified
everywhere: pedals, handlebars, axles and
steel tubing.

A nineteen-year-old YOUNG MAN is dressed in
overalls, and he whistles as he works, taping
the grips of the handlebars and fitting the
stems. The YOUNG MAN is deep in concentration
when there is a loud yell and a machine
squeals over the other side of the room.

WORKER ONE
(*yelling*)
Help! He's trapped, get help!

YOUNG MAN runs over. Everyone is gathered
around. Most of the men are older than him,
experienced workers, but some can't look
and some are panicking. There is a lot of
blood. Someone has pressed the emergency
stop button on the machine, but nobody is
attending to the injured man.

YOUNG MAN
(*urgently*)
Shut off all the machines! Do it, now!
Someone call an ambulance.

Men scatter, and the groans and clunks of
the surrounding machinery slowing down and
shutting off commence until the factory
floor is quiet. Except for the trapped and
injured man groaning in pain.

YOUNG MAN moves closer and sees the man's
hand and forearm is caught in the jaws of a
cutting machine. His eyes are rolling with
pain but he is slumping and making less
noise. The injured man continues groaning,
with incoherent whispers.

YOUNG MAN
What's that, my friend?

WORKER ONE
(*calls from sidelines*)
You'll not be able to understand him, he's
foreign.

WORKER TWO

I knew he'd be trouble, soon as they took
him on.

YOUNG MAN

(*annoyed*)

We don't need to understand him to help him,
you bloody idiots. Where's that ambulance?

WORKER TWO

Oi, watch your mouth, young 'un.

FOREMAN

Stand back now, help is almost here. Take a
five-minute break, you lot.

YOUNG MAN walks to canteen. He starts
chatting to the NEW LAD next to him in the
queue. They are both around the same age.

YOUNG MAN

I haven't seen your face before. Are you
new? I haven't been working here that long
myself.

NEW LAD

Aye. My dad works here. He got me the job.

The NEW LAD does not look happy to be there.

                    YOUNG MAN
You'll be all right here, you know. You can
               earn a good wage.

                     NEW LAD
                    (*eagerly*)
   I'd rather be writing, but my dad says
that's not a proper job. One day it will be,
though. In a few years, I'll be a published
               writer, you'll see.

                    YOUNG MAN
 I like reading. Maybe I'll read one of your
   books. What sort of things do you write
                      about?

                     NEW LAD
                    (*shrugs*)
    People like us, places like this.

YOUNG MAN looks sideways at him. He
hesitates, looks as if he's trying to make
his mind up whether to give him a bit of
advice or not.

                        255

YOUNG MAN
(*kindly*)
I hope your dream comes true, I really do.
But if you want my advice, it's to write
about something a bit more interesting. I
mean, why would folks want to read about
people like us and places like *this*?

He looks around him gloomily at the busy
canteen.

NEW LAD smiles, as if the answer is obvious.

NEW LAD
(*looking around in awe*)
Because this is *real life*, that's why. What
could be more interesting than that?

YOUNG MAN
(*sighs*)
It's up to you, but don't say I didn't
warn you. I can't imagine anyone would
want to read a book about ordinary folk that
work at the Raleigh factory. Good luck to
you, though.

END SCENE.

★

Sergei spends the next hour getting me to the bathroom, helping me back into my baggy tracksuit bottoms and a clean T-shirt.

I try out the crutches that Dad collected, but it's still too painful for me to manage on my own.

In the end, I manage to get to the living room using one crutch and leaning heavily against Sergei.

He pushes open the door with his free arm and I see that the room is dim. The curtains are still closed.

Then I see it, standing next to my chair.

Tall and sleek and lit up from the inside.

'For you, my friend,' Sergei says. 'This model is one I make for your very special day.'

It's a perfect replica of The Shard.

I ask Sergei not to open the curtains for a while, and we sit in the semi-gloom and look at the model that must have taken him hours to build. For me.

'Thanks, Sergei,' I say for the third time. 'The Shard is my favourite London landmark.'

'I know this,' he says. 'Now a little of The Shard belongs to you.'

I sit quiet and still, feeling the dull ache that ticks constantly backwards and forwards from my hip into my thigh and calf.

I listen to the noises of the street outside the window.

Car engines and children laughing. I can faintly hear Mr Baxter coughing downstairs.

Sergei sits quietly staring at The Shard, but I don't think he's really looking at it. Last night his mum rang to say his grandad was very ill but still putting up a fight. After the call Sergei went into the bedroom and when he came out his eyes looked sore.

'It must be hard,' I say. 'Being stuck here when you'd rather be somewhere else.'

'It is very difficult,' he says quietly. 'Nothing feels – how do you say – like things you are used to?'

'Familiar?' I suggest.

'That is it. Nothing in my life is *familiar*. There is just strangeness and trying to keep out of everyone's way who do not want us here.'

I swallow hard and nod.

'Is it so wrong to want a better life, Calum?'

'Course not,' I say.

'Things were not good at home, but things are not good here. It is not the new life Mama talked about.'

'Give it time,' I say. 'Things can change.'

I look at The Shard and imagine I am standing right at the very top of that last jagged slice, the bit that sits closest to the clouds. If I look up I can see the sky, if I look down I can see the Thames snaking its way through London town, past the buildings that must look like Lego models from this far up.

One day I will do it. I will stand at the top of The Shard, as far up as I can go, and I'll look down on all of London.

I've told myself this before, but somehow today feels different.

Today, I really believe I can do it.

I put on one of my favourite action movies, but I can tell Sergei is restless.

'Sometimes it is difficult to understand what is being said,' he complains. 'It makes watching the film very hard work when English is not your first language.'

I suppose I can understand that. The actors use a lot of slang and they speak really fast, too.

We have tinned tomato soup and bread for lunch, and when I hear Sergei washing the dishes in the kitchen, I pick up my notebook and pen.

I'm making slow progress but I'm getting on quite well with my screenplay. I'm thinking about stuff that happens on the estate and some of the people that live around here and feel stuck. I need to think of a place they would go and what they would do, if they believed they could achieve it.

Maybe Sergei fancies building something this afternoon. After seeing The Shard, I wouldn't mind watching how he does it, without falling asleep like last time.

At that moment he comes back in, wiping his wet hands on a tea-towel.

'Do you need anything else, Calum?'

'No, I'm good, ta,' I say, biting the end of my pen.

'I have to go out,' he says. 'I will be back soon.'

'Oh yeah, where are you off to?'

He half turns away from me and I can almost see the cogs whirring in his head.

'Nowhere important,' he murmurs. 'See you soon, yes?'

'You're always *just going out* for a couple of hours,' I say. 'Where is it you're going?'

'Here and there.' He shrugs. 'I do not have to report to you. You are not my teacher, Calum.'

'Sorry I asked.' I fold my arms in a huff.

My ribs still feel bruised from the accident, and folding my arms presses on to the sorest places, but I bite down on my tongue and don't let on it's hurting.

He walks past me and grabs his jacket off the chair. As he pushes an arm into his sleeve, a folded-up piece of paper drops at my feet, but he doesn't notice.

I open my mouth to tell him and then decide against it. He's acting like a prat, so why should I help him out? I slide my free foot to the side and cover up the paper. Hopefully it's something important that he needs. It will serve him right to lose it.

Sergei hangs back a moment and looks as though he

might say something else, but then thinks better of it and walks out of the room without speaking to me again. I hear him open and close the back door.

Where is he going that's such a big secret? It's so frustrating that I can't follow him. I reach down, my eyes watering with the effort of stretching through the stabbing pain that starts up in my hips.

It's agonizingly slow, but finally my fingers close on the paper and I sit back up and unfold it. At first glance it looks like some kind of hand-drawn plan – pencilled lines and boxes.

It's not until I fully unfold the paper that I realize what I'm looking at.

It's a floor plan of the Expressions community centre.

31

I snap awake, and look down to find my notebook and pen lying discarded in my lap.

I must have fallen fast asleep in my chair.

The back door rattles and opens, and I hear laughter and voices.

'Hello?' I call out.

Sergei appears in the doorway holding a large white box. I reach down with my hand and push the hand-drawn plan of the centre he dropped further down the gap between the seat cushion and the chair.

'So, how is the birthday boy?' Sergei turns and grins at someone who is standing just out of sight behind the door. Whoever it is lets out a snorting laugh. 'I have another surprise gift for you, Calum.'

He steps aside and the concealed person does a star jump into his place.

'Ta-dah!'

It is Amelia.

I'm surprised how pleased I am to see her, so at first I smile.

And then I remember I can't move, I've not showered

for the last three days, and the flat is in even more of a mess than usual. And it looks like the beaming Sergei in front of me is involved in some way with the theft and damage at Expressions. So I frown.

'What are you doing here?'

'Nice welcome,' Amelia barks. 'Cheers for that.'

'I didn't mean . . .' I look at Sergei. 'How come you've contacted Amelia?'

As far as I know, they've only met that once, at the community centre.

'I thought this would be a nice birthday surprise for you, Calum.' Sergei looks pleased with himself. 'You talk all the time about Amelia and *My Fair Lady*, and Amelia's hair, her eyes . . .'

'Yes, yes, all right, I get the picture.'

Sergei's making me sound a proper loser. *As if* I've been mooning over Amelia – I might've mentioned her once or twice in passing but . . .

'Aww, Calum, I didn't know you cared.' Amelia's face lights up in a mischievous grin. She rushes over and sits on the arm of my chair, and plants a kiss on my cheek. 'Happy birthday, matey.'

'Thanks.' I fan my burning cheeks with my hand.

'Sorry, I haven't got you a card.' She pulls a sad face.

''S'all right,' I say with a shrug.

That's the least of my worries. I brush bits of fluff off my legs. I bet my hair is sticking up all over the place.

'I got you something even better than a card.' She beckons Sergei into the room and takes the white box from him. 'Happy birthday, Calum.'

She places the box lightly on my aching knees and I open it.

Inside is a chocolate cake decorated with silver stars. Two unlit candles sit on the top in the shape of numbers: a one and a five.

I can't remember ever having a proper birthday cake like this. It's not the sort of thing that would occur to Dad. And Mum's been gone for so many birthdays now, I don't know if she ever got me one.

'Thanks, Amelia,' I say over-brightly, to try and cover up the sudden prickle in my eyes. 'It's great, really great.'

'Me and Spike helped Ma make it this morning,' she beams, lifting the cake carefully out of the box. 'I made the stars from marzipan and Spike hand-painted them with proper food colouring.'

Sergei produces a tray and Amelia lowers the cake on to it.

They light the candles, then – and this is the worst bit – they sing 'Happy Birthday' to me while my cheeks burn and Amelia takes photos on her phone despite my yells of disapproval about how scruffy I look.

'And finally,' Amelia announces, 'I got you this!'

She produces a DVD case and thrusts it in my hands.

'*Billy Elliot*. I've heard of this film,' I say doubtfully.

The boy on the cover is jumping in mid-air with a pair of ballet shoes around his neck. I don't want to appear ungrateful, but I'm not into dancing.

'It's a musical now, too. Ma took me and Spike to see it last year and we loved it.'

'What is this film about?' Sergei asks.

'Ballet dancing, I think.' I keep my voice level.

'It is and it isn't about dancing.' Amelia shrugs. 'It's set in the 1984 miners' strike and it's about a boy who follows his dream. Everybody loves it because we all have dreams – Billy's just happens to be dancing.'

I read the blurb and find it's set in Northumberland and Newcastle. It sounds like Billy has a battle on his hands to follow his dream, despite his bullying older brother and his bad-tempered dad trying to stop him. I can see a connection with *Kes*; it seems to have that authentic, real-life feel to it that I discussed with Freya.

'Thanks, Amelia,' I say. 'I'll definitely watch it.'

Sergei disappears into the kitchen to get a knife and plates. When I'm certain he's out of hearing range, I whisper to Amelia.

'Write down your phone number for me before you go. I need you to do something.'

Her face lights up. 'Ooh, sounds exciting. What is it?'

I glance at the doorway but I can still hear Sergei rooting around in the cutlery drawer.

'Sergei's up to something.' I frown. 'I need you to

follow him tomorrow afternoon, see where he goes.'

We don't get the chance to talk any more because Sergei stays in the room all the time. But later, after Amelia has left, I manage, through a series of texts, to convince her to hang around the end of our street early tomorrow afternoon to follow Sergei.

Or at least I *think* I've convinced her, until I get another text:

I've decided I don't want to do this. I like Sergei, it feels mean. A

My heart sinks. I'm not strong enough yet after the accident to follow Sergei, and there's nobody else I can ask.

Then, right on cue, Sergei puts his head around the door and announces he's going to take a bath.

Perfect.

It seems forever listening to the water running, until I finally hear him close the bathroom door.

I dial Amelia's number.

'You have to do it,' I hiss down the phone.

'Actually, I don't have to do anything,' she replies coolly.

'Please,' I say. 'This is important.'

'Why? It's none of your business if Sergei wants to go out somewhere without telling you what he's up to.'

'I think he might be the one damaging the community centre on the estate,' I tell her. 'There's been loads of

266

vandalism there lately and it seems to be happening when Sergei goes missing for the afternoon.'

There: I said it. The line goes quiet.

'I don't know for sure,' I add. 'That's why I need your help.'

'You've got to be kidding me,' Amelia says slowly. 'Sergei wouldn't do anything like that.'

'How do you know? You only just met him.'

'I'm a good judge of people,' she says. 'I don't think for a minute he's the sort of person who would—'

'I found something he dropped, OK? It was a plan of the centre he'd sketched. Why would he do that?'

She sighs, and I imagine her shaking her head and her bunched black curls straining to escape from the spotted red ribbons.

'If the vandalism continues, the centre could close,' I tell her.

'And that would be the end of the screenwriting competition,' Amelia remarks.

'It's not just that,' I say. But that's part of it.

I instruct Amelia to hang back when she's shadowing Sergei. 'Don't get too close.'

'D'ya think I'm thick or something?' she snaps. 'You didn't see me that day I followed you to the Arboretum after school, did you?'

'What?'

She followed *me*?

'You've been snooping on me?'

'Don't get excited; you're not that interesting,' she answers. 'Me and Mum were cycling past the end of the road when we saw you turn into the Arboretum, that's all. I wanted to come and say hi but we had to get back to the boat for Spike.'

Amelia was full of surprises.

32

I don't know how I manage to convince her, but in the end Amelia reluctantly agrees to follow Sergei the next day.

I sit in my chair, the excitement seeming to slightly dull the aching waves travelling up and down my leg. My bruised ribs are throbbing, too. Later, when Sergei gets out of the bath, it will be time for my painkillers, and I'm counting the minutes.

But in the meantime, I think about what might happen tomorrow.

I've seen someone suspicious twice now at the centre.

As I told Shaz, the centre manager, both times there had been a lone figure lurking around the side where the bins are.

I can't think of why Sergei would be interested in stealing or vandalizing the place, but that's beside the point. Maybe he's bored, or jealous of me entering the screenwriting competition . . . Who knows?

One thing that's certain: he keeps mysteriously disappearing off somewhere, and then we hear that the centre has been vandalized again.

Then he doesn't turn up at the school gates and

I get run over outside the centre.

Surely that's too much of a coincidence?

'That feels much better.' Sergei walks over to my chair, his hair still damp from the bath. 'There is nothing quite as good as a long soaking in the bath, yes?'

'Yeah.'

Especially if you're hot and dusty from breaking windows.

'Here are your tablets, Calum. I hope you are not in too much pain.'

'Thanks.' I take the tablets and wash them both down with a gulp of water.

'Mama has rung to say Dziadek is a little better today. Good news, yes?'

'Very good news,' I agree. 'I'm glad.'

'Are you hungry? I can make you a snack if you would like?'

'Nah, I'm fine, thanks.'

'A hot drink, perhaps?'

I wish he'd stop being so nice. Tomorrow I might have to shop him to the police.

'What did you get up to when you went out earlier today, then?' I ask him. Obviously he saw Amelia, but he was gone a few hours before returning to the flat with her.

'Ah . . . you know. This and that, I think you say.'

Annoyingly non-committal, as usual. 'What about you?'

'Oh, I ran a couple of laps around the park, went down the gym. Just the usual.'

'Ha! I think you are tricking with me, Calum.' He grins.

'There's no fooling you,' I remark drily.

'I mean to say, have you been reading your book and writing your screenplay for the community centre competition?'

'I might have.' I narrow my eyes at him. 'Why are you suddenly so interested?'

Sergei sighs and holds out his hands, palms up.

'It seems I am saying the wrong thing. I am just trying to make tiny talk, that is all.'

'*Small* talk,' I correct him. 'Not *tiny* talk.'

'Ah yes, of course.' He grins again. 'I hope you have had a nice birthday even though your father is not here, Calum.'

'Yeah, thanks. I have.'

Despite my suspicions, I mean it. Just a few days ago, I hated the thought of sharing the flat with Sergei and his mum. I'd got so used to always being on my own when Dad was working, and I longed for it to just be the two of us again.

But I've found that having other people around isn't all bad. I smile to myself, thinking about Amelia, and her chocolate cake and film gifts.

I look over at The Shard and wonder how many hours Sergei must've spent building it. That funny birthday card that's way too young for me and how he went to the trouble to find Amelia and bring her here to surprise me.

I shift about a bit in my seat but it's inside that I feel most uncomfortable. The way I've treated people.

'It is amazing, isn't it, that whatever you can see, it began as an idea in someone's mind,' Sergei says, staring at The Shard. 'The cars outside, the books we read, the clothes we wear, and all the buildings we live in – they all began life as an *idea*.'

'Suppose so.' I shrug. I'd never thought about it, but now he comes to mention it, my screenplay is beginning to grow from an idea.

'I think it is an amazing thing,' Sergei says, looking around the room. 'Everything I can see here was once only an idea. When you realize this fact, it frees you up to do anything you like, Calum.'

'Does it?' I yawn.

'Yes. Because you are realizing that an idea is the important first stage to creating something. Think about it. Your writing idea may one day become a film that lots of people come to watch and enjoy. Perhaps one day I may build my own skyscraper, one that towers above the city of Warsaw and is even higher than The Shard.'

He's living in a dream world.

'Yeah, well, it's a nice idea, but people like us don't get to do stuff like that.'

'People like us?'

'Ordinary working-class people who live in places like this.' I sweep my hand around to take in the flat, the street, the entire grimy estate.

'I think you will find *people like us* can achieve a lot of things, Calum,' he says. 'All we have to do is believe it is so.'

I've had enough of his funny ideas now, so I scowl and shrug, and he gets the message and finally shuts up and leaves.

But then I can't stop thinking about Barry Hines and how he must've had an idea for a book that he eventually wrote. A book that then became *Kes*, probably the best film I have ever seen.

I have a good idea for a play about ordinary people. It's just the belief in my writing ability that is missing.

I sit for a while, misery burning at my insides like acid. There has to be something I can do to stop feeling this helpless. Suddenly life is something that happens to everyone else while I sit here festering in the armchair.

I look down at my legs. They look the same as they ever did in my tracky bottoms, but it feels like somebody else's limbs have been stuck into my hip sockets. One bangs and thumps with pain, the other feels weak and useless. But then, I suppose, looking on the bright side, my legs didn't let me down. They hung on in there and now they're trying to heal and get back to being useful. The least I can do is try and help them along.

I shuffle to the end of my chair cushion, which feels like old Chopin battering them all over again. Then I reach across, stretching my arm to the limit until I touch one of my crutches that's leaning against the settee.

Slowly and painfully I wriggle, until I manage to grasp the crutch. I use it to hook the other one and pull it over to me. I have them both now, in my lap. I sit for a couple of minutes trying to get my breath back and cool down a bit before the real torture begins: trying to stand up.

I push down on the crutches, trying to lever myself up from the chair. Apart from giving me more excruciating stabbing pains in my thigh, it has no effect.

I try propping the crutches up against my seat, grasping the arms of the chair and using the strength in my arms to get me to a standing position. I grab one crutch and then the other.

It takes me a good five minutes to get them both in place under each arm, but I do it.

I haven't got the energy or the pain threshold to take a single step forward, but I'm standing.

At last, I'm standing on my own two feet again.

33

I'm tetchy from the moment I wake up.

No, I tell Sergei, I don't want breakfast.

No, I don't want a shower or a clean set of clothes. I'll wear my old tracky bottoms and the ripped T-shirt again.

'What have you got planned for today then?' I ask him.

I'm trying to sound casual but I think I might sound nervous and unusually inquisitive.

'Just the usual things.' He looks at me. 'We could build a model together this morning, if you wish?'

My heart blips. What if he doesn't go out as planned?

'What about this afternoon?' I suggest.

'This morning is better,' Sergei replies. 'Later, I have to go out for a short time.'

It looks like everything's going to plan, after all. Later today Amelia will find out what it is Sergei is up to, where it is he's going every afternoon. And if it turns out he is responsible for the vandalism at the centre, well, then . . . I'll have to tell Dad. And Dad will have a duty to tell Shaz and the police. That's the unavoidable truth.

And then . . . well, I'm not sure. I haven't really

thought what might happen after that.

Sergei and Angie might get deported. The authorities could send them back to Poland, I suppose. Back to a potentially dangerous situation with Sergei's violent father. That might happen anyway, depending on what happens with Brexit.

I don't really want to think about all the stuff that could happen in the future.

I squeeze my eyes closed and try to get my thoughts in line again.

If Sergei is the culprit, if he's damaging the centre, he will have to face the consequences. That's the way stuff works here. It will be nobody else's fault but his own. Everything will go back to normal for me and Dad. I'll get my bedroom back and all my space.

Sergei will take his buildings with him, except for The Shard. He can't take that because he's already given it to me as a gift. My mind fills with memories of life before Sergei and Angie came to live here.

The cool silence that hit me like an invisible wall the second I got in after school. Dad's constant and unchanging expression: mouth down-turned, cheeks sagging, permanent frown. He'd come home from working away all week, heavy on his feet, fast asleep by nine o'clock in front of the TV.

He hasn't been like that at all since the Zurakowskis arrived. Dad seems more alive, more energized, somehow.

He's always laughing and he's not staying away from home as much.

But Sergei misses Poland, he's said so. He has also said, many times, how much he misses his grandad and his school friends. If I focus on that, the heaviness in my heart might start to fade.

Sergei suggests building another model together, but I say I feel too tired.

I can't concentrate on anything, even my screenplay. I keep thinking about what Amelia will discover when she follows him this afternoon.

Beans on toast for lunch, then Sergei seems to be in the kitchen for ages, cleaning up. At last he comes into the room with his jacket on.

'Is there anything you need, Calum?'

'No thanks, I'm good.'

'OK, I am going out for a while. I will see you soon.'

'See you later,' I call.

Soon as the back door closes behind him, I text Amelia.

He's just left. Where are you?

Amelia's reply is instant.

Corner of next street. Over and out. A

Very funny. Amelia seems to be treating this as a bit of a joke, and it isn't.

After that, I don't hear anything. At all.

I try and read through the first scene of my screenplay,

but after the third time of reading the first couple of lines, I give up. I don't feel anything when I read it . . . It needs to feel – I don't know – more *real*. I grab my crutches and manage to stand up again, but I'm still unable to take even a step forward without collapsing down in the chair.

I bite each one of my nails in turn, and I close my eyes to try and take a nap, but of course that proves impossible.

Then I get a text.

On my way back to yours. A

I send three texts back asking stuff like: Did Sergei go to the centre? Where is he now? How long will you be?

Amelia ignores them all.

I have no option but to sit and wait.

I scratch at a mark on the tweedy material that covers the armchair. I go through the first scene of the screenplay again. I bite my already severely bitten fingernails. I look out of the window at the roofs of the houses on the opposite side of the road.

After the longest thirty minutes in history, the back door opens.

'It's only me,' calls Amelia.

This is it. This is where I get to find out what Sergei is up to, where I have to break the bad news to Dad, and then Shaz, and finally to the police. There'll be no more Sergei and Angie in the flat, just me and Dad again.

'Hello?!' Amelia waves her hand in front of my face. 'Earth to Planet Brooks?'

'Sorry,' I say. 'I was just thinking.'

She sighs and sits down on the settee.

'So . . .' I start to babble. 'Did he go to the centre? Is Sergei breaking the windows?'

Amelia looks at me but her face is blank.

'Just tell me,' I snap. 'What's he up to?'

'I don't know,' Amelia replies.

'What do you mean, you *don't know*? Did you follow him?'

'Yes.'

'Did he see you?'

'No.' She rolls her eyes. 'I even managed to get the same bus as him without being spotted. I'm good at this stuff.'

'The bus?'

The centre is only five minutes' walk from here. Where could Sergei be going that involves a *bus* ride?

Amelia twists and untwists her fingers.

'I followed him to the Victoria Centre bus station. It was easy to stay hidden cos there were loads of people waiting for the buses. Sergei got on one and went straight upstairs so I sat downstairs, right at the back.'

'Go on,' I urge her.

'We were only on the bus about ten minutes when he comes back downstairs. Luckily a few people got off at his stop so I just stayed well behind them. The schedule screen on the bus said we were in Sherwood.'

'Sherwood?'

'Can you stop repeating everything I say?' Amelia snaps.

'Sorry.'

Sherwood wasn't far from here, but it's not a place I ever have reason to go to.

'So, he walks up this hill on the main street and I stay well behind. There are lots of shops and people around so it's not hard to stay hidden.'

'That's good,' I murmur. I'm trying not to rush her but I wish she'd stop dragging the story out.

'He turns into Perry Road. It's a really long road and there are fewer people about here so I have to hang right back. But he doesn't turn around.'

Perry Road. It sounds familiar for some reason, but I've never been there.

I stay quiet.

'Then, at the end of Perry Road, he takes a turn and just disappears.'

'You lost him?' I feel a rush of blood to my head.

'Calm down, Calum; I didn't lose him!' She scowls at me. 'But I can't see where he's gone at first because I'm hanging back, remember?'

'Yeah, course, sorry,' I mumble.

'Anyway, when I catch up I see what this place is. I

see Sergei pressing a buzzer and waiting at the big gates to be let in.'

'Did you manage to follow him in?' I envisage a big house with electric gates. Who does Sergei know who lives in a place like that? He's never mentioned anyone, but I know there are people around who have made an awful lot of money through criminal activities. Maybe it was the head of some crime syndicate that's come over here from Eastern Europe.

'No. I couldn't follow him,' Amelia says slowly.

I throw my hands up in frustration.

'I couldn't follow him in because he went into the *prison*,' Amelia whispers. 'They opened the doors for him and he walked right in there.'

34

'Nottingham Prison?' My mouth falls open. 'Why on earth would he be going *there*?'

'Going where?' A voice from the doorway makes us both jump.

'Sergei!' Amelia exclaims, and stands up. Then she sits down again. All her confidence has evaporated.

'The back door was wide open,' he says. 'You two look very worried. What has happened?'

Amelia and I look at each other.

'I'd better get going . . .' Amelia stands up.

'No – don't go,' I say.

'Sorry, I've got to; I told Ma I'd only be an hour. She needs me to look after Spike while she goes up to the boatyard for some spares.'

And in a flash Amelia has gone.

I look at Sergei. The ordinary boy who turns out to have a secret life of crime.

'Why are you looking at me in this way, Calum?' He frowns. 'As if you have not seen me before . . . as if I am a stranger.'

I shake my head, not knowing where to start.

'Is Amelia upset about something?' Sergei looks

concerned. 'I hope she is OK.'

'Yeah, she's fine,' I say, glaring at him. 'She's just had a bit of a shock. A big shock, actually.'

Sergei sits down and stares at me.

'You also look as if you have had a bit of a shock, my friend.'

'Sergei, you can lose the act now. I know where you've been going,' I say, keeping my voice calm and level. 'I know you've been to the prison today and I'm assuming that's where you've been going in the afternoons. There's no point in denying it.'

The colour drains from his face in an instant, and then flushes back into his cheeks in the form of two little round hot spots.

'Amelia. She has followed me,' he growls.

'Yes, she did,' I say, hoping I sound more confident than I feel. 'She had to because you wouldn't tell me where you were going and I thought it was you who'd been . . .'

He opens his eyes wide.

'Well, I thought you might have been going to the centre.'

His whole face seems to darken.

'You thought I was the one causing the damage there?' He whispers the words, his features squeezing together as if he can't quite get his head around this fact.

'No, but . . . I didn't know, did I? Because you wouldn't tell me—'

'I don't have to tell you where I am going, Calum. It does not mean I am causing the vandal damage.'

I want to correct him to say 'vandalism', but from the way he's looking at me, and the fact I can't even move on my own yet, I decide against it.

'And I found the plan you'd drawn of the centre. Why would you do that?'

'I wondered if you would prefer a building of the Expressions centre instead of The Shard for your birthday, Calum. It was a silly idea but I thought it would encourage you to enter the competition.' He looks deflated. 'I showed your father my plan to see if he could help me to build it, but he said you loved The Shard more.'

'I'm sorry,' I say. And I mean it. 'But why are you going to the prison? Who do you know there?'

For a second he frowns harder, and I think he's going to tell me to mind my own business. But then he kind of shrinks a bit and sits with his elbows on his knees and his head in his hands.

'Sergei?' I say gently, and he looks up, tears streaking his pale cheeks.

'It is my brother Janusz,' he says softly. 'He is stuck inside the prison. He has been there a while.'

*

I'm speechless with shock. I stay quiet and let Sergei tell me in his own time.

'He came to England a year ago, just before myself and Mama. He had left our little house in search of a better life,' Sergei explains, looking at his hands. 'He got a job on a building site and made some friends. One night in the pub some youths set upon his English friend, Robert. They said Robert had been staring at one of their girlfriends.'

His breathing gets faster, more shallow, but I stay quiet.

'Janusz tried to defend his friend but they would not listen. When one of the men tried to hit Robert with a baseball bat from behind, Janusz pushed him hard, out of the way. The man fell and hit his head on the corner of the metal counter. The police came in a big van and took Janusz away.'

I can't think what to say.

'Janusz got convicted of assault and the court gave him a two-year prison sentence. But the English men who attacked Robert stayed free. I ask you, Calum, where is the justice in that?'

'I-it doesn't sound like there's any justice in it at all,' I stammer, trying to process everything he's saying.

A crawling sensation starts on my scalp. *Does Dad know about Janusz?*

I think about the day I heard Sergei and his mum

whispering in Polish to each other in the kitchen. What if she has kept it from Dad for some reason?

'I visit him three times during the week, and Mama goes each weekend. It is making her very sad.'

'Has she told my dad?' I ask him. 'About what happened to Janusz?'

His face goes a bit red and he doesn't answer for a few seconds.

'She is going to tell him very soon. It would have been done by now, but of course then Dziadek fell ill and Mama had to go—'

'She should've told Dad before that,' I say. 'Before you both moved in. He's got a right to know about something so serious.'

The crawling sensation has covered my arms and reached my hands now, and I scratch madly at my fingers. Angie seems to really like Dad, but what if she hasn't said anything about Janusz because she just needed a place to stay that's near to Nottingham Prison? Then I remember Dad's dodgy dealings in counterfeit handbags and how he told Sergei and me not to mention his 'last' work trip abroad to her.

'I beg you not to say anything to your father until Mama returns, Calum,' Sergei says anxiously. He stands up and shakes his hands like they're wet and he's trying to air-dry them. 'She cares very much for your father and she would not want to make him angry.'

'He probably *will* be angry,' I say, scowling at Sergei. 'I mean, wouldn't you be? It's not nice, being lied to.'

I expect him to shrink back at my words but he grows bolder and scowls back.

'It is not nice being accused of doing the vandal damage, either,' he snaps. 'It is not nice that you think this of me, Calum. Why do you never trust anyone to be a good person? Why do you always expect the worst of them, especially if they come from a different country?'

I open my mouth to shout back at him but I don't actually have anything I can say to defend myself. Angie herself has shown me nothing but kindness, and yet in seconds I have managed to think the worst of her.

I can't feel angry at Sergei's words because he's surprised me into realizing something that's true: I just don't trust people.

Mum's face drifts into my mind. I can't remember her much because I was so young back then. But I know she left me, and she left Dad, too.

You should be able to trust your own mum when you're so small. Trust that she'll be there forever, no matter what.

If your mum can leave you all alone, who is left to trust?

My face feels hot and my leg is banging with pain as if it's punishing me for being such an idiot. I look at the carpet in front of me and wish it was quicksand so it could just swallow me whole.

Sergei stands up and walks towards me. He looks as if he's going to slap me round the head or threaten me. There's nothing I can do about it in this state; maybe I even deserve it.

I steel myself for what's coming, but he knocks me out in a whole different way. His face softens and he lays his hand on my shoulder.

'Calum,' he says simply. 'You are my friend.'

My chest bucks as I try and hold in a sudden sob that comes from nowhere. I look away and blink furiously before I make a complete fool of myself.

I think of everything Sergei has done for me while I recover from the accident, how he has always forgiven me the awful things I've said to him and brushed aside the fact I've been part of a group that has mercilessly bullied him at school.

And it's at that moment that I realize something for the first time.

Sergei Zurakowski *is* my friend.

He's probably the best friend I've ever had.

35

Sergei is in the kitchen, making lunch.

I glance at my phone on the arm of the chair and see that I have a voicemail message. I left it on silent so didn't hear it ring.

The voicemail is from Dad.

'*I'm back later today. Listen, I've got to bring the stuff back to the flat, just overnight. It'll be gone again tomorrow but I wanted to say, no more wisecracks about it being illegal in front of Sergei, OK? We don't want to worry Angie about all this. See you later.*'

By 'the stuff' I assume Dad means his haul of fake handbags. He's never brought anything like that back to the flat before. I know it's risky. If the police catch him with it here, they could prosecute him.

I decide not to mention it to Sergei.

'Dad's coming back later today,' I tell him when he brings the sandwiches through.

He nods. 'There is something I would like to show you this afternoon, Calum. Something I would like you to see.'

'Fine,' I say with a shrug, wondering what building he's planning on making this time.

After we've eaten, Sergei helps me over to the settee and settles his mum's laptop on his knees so we can both see.

'I want to show you Warsaw, my home.'

I don't really feel like looking at some scabby little village with no running water or electricity. There are other things I need to think about, like how I'm going to tell Dad that Angie has an older son called Janusz that he didn't know about and who is currently banged up in Nottingham Prison for assault.

Sergei is my friend, but my dad . . . Well, family is family, right?

Sergei pulls up a photo on the screen. It shows a sprawling city at night. There is a big square with a tall monument in the centre. Little market stalls lit by tiny lanterns line the side streets, and the whole area is surrounded by beautiful buildings, most of them tall, with many floors and windows. The buildings are painted in different colours – terracotta, cream and green.

I point to a stunning building on the right with a clock tower and curved ornate decoration.

'Ah, this is one of my favourite buildings also, Calum,' he beams. 'Zamek Królewski, the Royal Castle. It was built in the fourteenth century. Now there are many concerts held here, and some wonderful art inside.'

Sergei flicks through photo after photo, showing stunning architecture, a university, a presidential palace.

I shake my head slowly in amazement. 'I thought you came from a little town with hardly anything but squirrels there.'

Sergei laughs out loud. 'There are approximately two point seven million people living in Warsaw. It is hardly a tiny town. Much bigger than Nottingham.'

He tells me that most of Warsaw was flattened to rubble during the war and had to be completely rebuilt. That's hard to imagine, looking at the impressive skyline there now.

'But there is more to Warsaw than buildings. We have many forests there, too,' Sergei adds, proudly showing me photographs of him and Angie sitting at a small cafe table, surrounded by trees. 'And here is the Chopin monument at the Royal Lazienki Park.' He points to another shot of himself posing proudly beside it.

He clicks on another photograph, and when it loads up he's struck silent for a few seconds.

'And this . . .' he says softly. 'This is home.'

It is a small, neat house on the edge of a pine forest. Sergei, Angie and a grizzled old man stand together outside.

'This is Dziadek.' He points to the old fella and his voice softens. 'Our neighbour took the photograph just before Mama and I left to come to England.'

They are all smiling in the photo, but I know from what Sergei told me that it must have been a very scary time. They were all afraid of his father and what he might do next.

Sergei is showing me some photos of his best friend, Pawel, when we hear a noise at the back door.

'Hello,' Angie calls. 'Surprise, I am home!'

She's not supposed to be back yet. Dad is on his way with his illegal goods haul.

I hear her struggling in with her suitcase, and Sergei runs through to help her.

'How is he?' I hear him ask breathlessly as they drag luggage into the hall. 'How is Dziadek?'

'He is good, Sergei.' She smiles when they reach the living-room door. 'He is much better. I think he is going to be OK.'

Sergei hugs her, then turns to look at me, and I grin and give him the thumbs-up. His eyes linger on me a bit longer. He's wondering if I'm going to tell Angie I know that Janusz is in prison.

'And how are you, Calum?' Angie walks over to me. 'Are you also getting better?'

'Yeah, thanks,' I say. 'My leg is still really painful but Sergei's a great nurse.'

'Ha!' Angie laughs. 'Perhaps this is your calling in life, Sergei. Not to become an architect of great buildings but a *nurse*.'

Sergei shakes his head, and grins, but his eyes keep darting at me, unsure of what I'll do next.

I reach for my phone. I need to let Dad know Angie is home.

I text Dad several times but there's no reply.

When Angie and Sergei are busy in the kitchen, I ring him. There's no ring tone, it just goes straight to answerphone, which must mean the phone is off or he's in an area of poor signal.

I've decided I'm not going to mention the Janusz situation to Dad by phone. Best to wait until he's home.

But they'll have to tell him as soon as he gets back. It's only right.

Angie comes into the room and I know immediately, by the look on her face, that Sergei has told her I know about Janusz.

'I am sorry you had to hear the news about my eldest son from someone else, Calum,' she says, her eyes downcast.

'It's just . . . Dad. My dad should know about him.'

'Of course.' Angie nods, her eyes shining. 'I should have told him right away, I know that. It is just that there was never a good time and I admit I was afraid he would tell us to go, to leave. And I really don't want to leave, because I love your father, Calum.'

Blimey. This is all getting a bit too intense.

I shuffle uncomfortably in my chair and stare at my phone screen.

Angie seems to sense I'm embarrassed and goes into the kitchen. I send another couple of texts to Dad, but he still doesn't reply.

An hour later, Sergei and I sit in the lounge while Dad and Angie are arguing in the kitchen over what Sergei says is a mountain of black bin bags filled with fake handbags.

'I just don't understand why you are dealing with criminals, Pete,' I hear Angie cry out. 'You are a talented man who can rely on his own hard work and skills to make money. And you could go to prison.'

A deathly silence falls in the kitchen. Sergei and I glance at each other.

And then Angie tells Dad. She tells him all about Janusz.

36

Dad and Angie disappear into the bedroom 'to talk'.

Sergei listens at the door for a while, but all he says he can hear are the odd few heated words and his mum sobbing.

After seeing Angie, and how upset she was about not telling Dad the truth, I believe what she says is true. That there was just never a good time to talk about Janusz. Just like there was never a good time to tell Linford that Sergei had moved in with us.

I believe Angie is a good person. I trust her.

'Don't worry, they'll sort it out,' I tell Sergei, noticing how quiet he is. 'Everything will be OK, you'll see.'

'I was just thinking about something, Calum. There is something important we still do not know the answer to.'

'What's that?'

'You still have your mystery to be solved.' He looks at me. 'If I am not the person vandalizing the centre, then who is?'

I nod. 'And there's the even bigger mystery of who was driving the car that mowed me down in broad daylight.'

Dad says the centre is probably going to have to close

after this latest damage, and somewhere there's a crazy driver who is still loose behind the wheel.

'Why don't we just camp out there?' I'm suddenly filled with bravado. 'We could hang around every afternoon until we find out what's happening.'

Sergei's eyes drift to my legs.

'You can push me in the wheelchair,' I urge him. 'And we won't do anything stupid. We'll call the police if anything kicks off, maybe get a picture on my phone as evidence. What do you say? We've nothing else to do with our time.'

Sergei's face lights up.

'We can begin tomorrow afternoon.' He grins. 'Maybe we can ask Amelia to help us. I think she could keep a secret.'

Later, Dad and Angie come out of the bedroom and sit side by side on the settee.

Sergei and I stop sorting through the pieces of card required to build his latest project, the Eiffel Tower, and look at them both.

'We just wanted you to know everything is fine between us,' Dad says, reaching for Angie's hand. 'I understand why it was so hard for Angie to tell me about Janusz. Do you understand that too, Calum?'

'Yep.' I nod. 'Totally.'

Angie takes a deep breath as if she's steeling herself.

'Sergei and I want you to know, Pete and Calum, that we respect you and we are sorry for keeping this information from you.'

Angie looks at Dad, and smiles, and he kisses her on the cheek.

Sergei looks at me and smiles, and I smile back. But he's not getting a kiss. He grins like he knows what I'm thinking.

'We feel bad missing Calum's birthday,' Dad says, looking at me. 'So when you feel up to it, son, we're going to have a couple of nights in London to celebrate. All four of us.'

'Wow, thanks,' I say. Dad's *never* done anything like that for my birthday before and I don't know whether to believe him or not.

I look at Angie, and she gives me a secret wink. I know she's telling me it will happen.

Dad goes to the chippy and we all sit in the lounge. When we've finished eating and chatting about what we'll do in London, Angie puts the TV on.

Dad is trying to watch the news headlines while Sergei takes him through the very lengthy process of how he built The Shard.

We just look like an ordinary family, having an ordinary evening in.

My chest feels warm and solid, like everything is going to be OK.

I sit and look out of the window. I can see the street from my chair. It's dusk now but our curtains are still open. The odd car comes down the street, but all the younger kids have gone inside, so there's no football on the road and no squealing and laughing.

A lone figure comes into view, someone wearing a zipped-up jacket with a hood, hands buried deep in his pockets. I watch as he crosses over the road and stops outside our gate.

He pulls off his hood so I can see his face and he looks straight up at our window.

He has a black eye and he looks thinner than I remember. Even though he is a long way from me, I think I can see something in his eyes that tells me he wishes things were different. He looks scared.

Without thinking, I raise my hand and nod.

And Linford waves back. Then he pulls his hood up and carries on walking down the street, cutting a lonely figure in the semi-dark.

37

I wake up to banging in the hallway outside my room. Sergei's bed is empty.

I sit up and rub my eyes.

'Hello?' I call.

The door opens and Dad puts his head round.

'Sorry to wake you, son. I'm just getting my tools together to put in the van.' Dad's face is grim. 'Someone broke nearly every window in the centre last night.'

My mouth drops open and I get this heavy feeling in my throbbing legs, like they're both filled with cement.

'Shaz had only just locked up, so it must've been just after nine, because neighbours called the police at nine thirty.' Dad shakes his head in frustration. 'I'm off now to board up, so see you later, son.'

'Bye, Dad,' I say quietly, lost in my own thoughts.

Dad was watching the *Ten O'Clock News* last night at about the same time I spotted Linford outside on the street.

Later, Dad and Angie go shopping, and Sergei helps me down the steps and into my wheelchair.

The agony of my injured leg heats me up from the inside and I feel like abandoning our plan to go to the centre.

'If you cannot manage it, do not worry, Calum,' Sergei says. 'We can go another day.'

But by the time I collapse down into the wheelchair at the bottom, I can't face going back up the steps again, so the decision is made.

As Sergei pushes, we talk. I tell him my suspicions about Linford.

'He is your friend, Calum; you know him well. Do you trust him?'

I don't reply, but of course the answer is no. I don't trust Linford one bit.

Sergei parks up my wheelchair just the other side of a low hedge that borders a patch of waste ground on the edge of the estate and directly next to the centre.

The gates are locked up and the main shutter is pulled down over the entrance door. The windows Dad boarded up last night look like sightless eyes. The centre looks quiet, and a bit creepy, but there is nobody suspicious around.

There's a shout behind us and we both jump, wondering if it's someone out to get us.

Amelia starts to run towards us, smiling and waving.

'I only just saw your text, Sergei,' she says, slightly

out of breath when she reaches us. 'The signal isn't very good on the boat.'

'Shh,' Sergei tells her. 'We need to stay quiet and out of sight.'

I grin at her. I'm glad she's here.

I haven't noticed until now that Sergei has a rucksack strapped to his back. He unbuckles it and pulls out sandwiches, cake and crisps.

'We forgot to have lunch at home before we left,' he explains.

'Ooh, good, I'm starving.' Amelia helps herself to a cheese sandwich without being asked.

My stomach has been churning all the way here, not through hunger, but from wondering if we will witness Linford causing more damage.

Sergei hands me a small bottle of water and I take a long swig.

'Not much happening,' I say with a shrug. 'We might as well have gone fishing in the canal for all the hours we'll probably sit here with nothing to do.'

'This is all very . . . exciting.' Amelia rolls her eyes. 'But we're a bit old to be playing spy games.'

'There!' Sergei hisses, and ducks down, bending his knees so his head is below the hedge.

I part the hedge and catch movement. Over by the bins.

'It looks like him,' I whisper, taking in his dark jeans

and hoody. 'It could be Linford.'

'He looks dodgy,' Amelia says, crunching a crisp near my ear.

The figure has his back to us, but his hoody is pulled up over his head, and only his jeans and trainers are visible. The outfit certainly looks very similar to what Linford was wearing last night.

The figure creeps around the side of the building, rattling the window boards Dad had secured.

'I think he is trying to find a way in,' Sergei whispers.

'What shall we do?' asks Amelia. 'We can shout, to stop him causing more damage?'

'No. We need to catch him in the act or else it's just our word against his,' I say.

I take out my phone and snap a couple of pics, but when I check them, all I can see are hedge leaves. As I look at the screen, my phone dies. I forgot to charge it last night.

The figure pulls at one of the boards and then looks around shiftily. He pulls something from a deep pocket. A crowbar.

'Ring the police,' Sergei hisses without looking at me.

'I can't, my phone just ran out of charge.'

Suddenly there is a loud thud, and a board pulls clean away from one of the windows.

Sergei stands upright.

'I am going over there,' he says, his face thunderous.

'No! Are you mad?' Amelia grabs his arm. 'He might turn on you.'

'Someone has to stop him,' Sergei says, shrugging her off. 'He will run off and you two must try and see his face.'

Before I can say another word, Sergei is off. He bolts over the fence and shouts, 'Hey!'

The figure turns around, but we still haven't got a good view of his features because of the hedge in front of us.

I can hear shouting, scuffling. I can't move, and Amelia is rooted to the spot with wide eyes. The frustration burns like acid in my throat. And then I see there are more figures appearing inside the centre yard; I don't know where they have come from.

'Oh no, Sergei's going to get hurt,' Amelia cries out, running towards them.

I let out a yell of fury, desperate to help Sergei and Amelia but unable to move my legs.

There's a screech of brakes as Dad's van pulls up by the waste ground, and out he jumps. When I look round, Mrs Brewster is barrelling down the road towards us.

'Are you OK, Calum, love? I told your dad you were stuck out here.' She leans a hand on my wheelchair and bends over, gasping for air.

Dad heads over to me.

'Dad! Sergei and Amelia are over there.' I point round

the side of the centre. 'Sergei caught someone breaking in and went over. Amelia followed, and now there are loads of them. They're outnumbered.'

In a jiffy Dad is inside the centre yard. Angie gets out of the van and runs over to me.

'We had to come back from our shopping trip because your dad left his wallet at the flat,' she says, manoeuvring my wheelchair around the hedge and next to the centre's wire fence. 'Mrs Brewster told us you and Sergei had been sitting out here for a long time.'

Thank goodness for Mrs Brewster and her MI5 eyes.

'Oh Lord, they're fighting!' Mrs Brewster clutches her chest. 'I'd better go and call the police.'

The youths split off and sprint up and over the fence.

I watch as Amelia sticks her foot out and trips someone up, and seconds later Dad has the culprit by the scruff of his neck and is pulling him away from the bins. As the figure twists round I get a full view of his face, which I recognize very well.

I've seen enough of him at school.

38

'Get your hands off me you, you imbecile!' Hugo Fox storms, trying to shake off Dad's grip. 'My father is a very important man around here and he knows some very influential people. You're going to regret—'

'Shut it,' Dad growls. 'Don't threaten me with your toffee-nosed friends in high places. You'll answer to the law like the rest of us, whoever your old man might be.'

'Mr Fox is his dad,' I say as Angie wheels my chair closer. 'My Head Teacher at school.'

Hugo turns, his face all screwed up and ready to have a go at me, but then the strangest thing happens. When he sees me, his face drains of all colour and he swallows hard.

'What?' I say, but he looks quickly away.

I shrug my shoulders at Dad. I can't figure out why Hugo is acting so weirdly all of a sudden.

'Look, I'm sure we can come to some arrangement,' he starts babbling to Dad. 'My father is a man of means. I know you people around here always need money, we can – oww!'

A muscle flexes in Dad's jaw. He pulls Hugo over to the wire fence so he is standing next to us.

'We mightn't have piles of cash on this estate, but most of us know what's right and wrong,' he tells Hugo between gritted teeth. 'So don't insult me with your corrupt little offers. The police can decide what's going to happen to you.'

My useless phone falls clean out of my hand.

As I watch Angie reach to scoop it up, Hugo shuffles his feet, and that's when I see them.

White trainers with a broad green-and-red stripe. And in the middle of the stripe sits a perfectly embroidered little gold bee.

I sit upright in shock, grimacing as a bolt of pain shoots through both my hips.

For a few seconds, in my head, I'm back there.

Lying in the road, the booming bass beat, the voices and the white training shoe next to my face.

The glistening shape that I couldn't process back then comes flooding back to me with crystal clarity. It was a little gold bee sitting on a green-and-red-striped trainer.

Things move fast after that.

The police arrive and I recognize one of them as being PC Bolton, who came to speak to me at the hospital. Dad explains how we caught Hugo in the act of breaking into the centre.

'The others scarpered but I kept hold of this one,' Dad says.

'Get your hands off me!' Hugo squirms.

'We'll take it from here, thank you, sir,' PC Bolton says.

Dad lets go of Hugo's arm.

'N-now, officer,' Hugo stammers. 'Thank goodness you're here. You need to arrest this thug—'

'Just a minute, young man.' PC Bolton frowns. '*I'll* decide what action is taken, not you.'

Hugo closes his mouth.

And that's when I tell them. About the trainer. The significance of the bee.

'Rubbish,' Hugo says, his voice lifting higher and higher as he speaks. 'Don't be ridiculous, this boy is deluded.'

'There's only one foolish boy here so far as I can see,' PC Bolton remarks.

A week later, PC Bolton sits down in our living room and shakes his head at Dad.

'Unbelievable. I'll be honest, we were looking at some of the unsavoury characters who live here, on the estate,' he says. 'We were convinced the culprits responsible for the hit-and-run incident and the vandalism of the Expressions centre would be residents of the estate.'

'That's understandable.' Dad shrugs. 'It just proves that where you live has no bearing on knowing right from wrong.'

'That's true, and there's a lesson in there somewhere,' PC Bolton agrees. 'The word unofficially was that the Expressions centre would secure some major funding, so Hugo decided he'd ruin its chances himself. He paid Linford Gordon to break the windows and steal essential equipment.'

'Did Hugo admit to driving the car?' I ask.

'Eventually, but not until the evidence was rock solid against him. He and his father maintained his innocence all along, but fortunately, in the end, someone did come forward with information and then we knew we had the right man.'

'So someone did see it happen!' I gasp.

PC Bolton shakes his head. 'This person wasn't actually there on the day, but he heard Hugo Fox and his friends talking about what happened and decided to come forward. A very unlikely source of help, I might add.'

'Are you allowed to tell us who it was?' I ask.

'Linford Gordon,' PC Bolton replies. 'He said you'd been friends for most of your lives until just recently. To his credit, even though Hugo and his thugs threatened him with violence to keep quiet, he decided to do the right thing by you, Calum.'

I'm dumbstruck. Linford!

'I can't believe Hugo Fox's trainers gave him away,' Dad comments.

'Not just any trainers though, Mr Brooks,' PC Bolton

says. 'Those trainers are a top designer brand and the little gold bee is a distinctive trademark. Nearly four hundred pounds a pair. Not your regular footwear around these parts.'

'Blimey.' Dad seems baffled.

'We found minute traces of Calum's blood on the sole of one of the trainers. We found the same on the chrome grille of Hugo Fox's vehicle, despite it having been obviously scrubbed up and cleaned.'

'But why?' I say, still not fully understanding. 'Why did they do it and why did they damage the centre?'

'Seems Hugo wanted the centre closed so the funding went to the place where he runs classes and it was them who promised to send him to a top drama facility in London if their bid was successful. So he teamed up with a few thugs from the estate.' PC Bolton shakes his head in disapproval. 'Seems these thugs convinced Linford to break a few windows for cash. He said he did it because his stepdad is out of work and his little sister had no money for her school lunches or new shoes.'

'Hugo Fox,' I whisper. 'Who'd have thought it.'

I'm guessing Hugo won't be coming into school to brag at any more of our assemblies.

39

'Calum, get up,' I hear Dad call from across the hallway. 'There's something in here for you.'

I woke up about ten minutes ago and I've been just lying here, thinking. I finished reading *A Kestrel for a Knave* last night, and it was so good it feels like a little chunk of me is missing now. But at least I still have the new book Sergei gave me to read.

I'm going to ask Sergei if he fancies nipping into school with me to one of Mr Ahmed's holiday library sessions. I bet he knows all about the author Alan Sillitoe.

But not today. Today we're all going to Amelia's for tea . . . on *My Fair Lady*. Amelia's mum, Sandy, broke her foot when she slipped off the deck just as they were about to cast off and move to their next port of call. Sandy got special permission to stay longer on the canal, but they'll be leaving next week. She did say something about trying to get a permanent mooring, though – so maybe one day they'll come back. I really hope they do.

Me and Sergei have strict instructions to Skype Amelia and Spike once a week without fail – providing she has an internet connection, of course. Sandy has invited us both to stay for a week on *My Fair Lady* on the Norfolk

Broads next year. We can't wait.

Before I leave my bedroom, there's something I have to do. Something I've been putting off because he'll probably tell me to get lost, or worse. But if he does, I reason, at least I'll know I tried.

I pick up my phone and scroll down to Linford's number. My finger hovers above the call button and, before I can change my mind, I press it.

He probably won't even answer anyway when he sees my name pop up on his screen.

After two rings, he picks up.

'Hello? Cal?'

'Yeah, it's me.'

I'd planned what to say, but now it all tumbles out anyhow and barely makes sense.

'I . . . I just wanted to say thanks. You know, for telling the police—'

'It wasn't right, what they did,' Linford says quickly. 'Hugo and his mates. I should've grassed them up earlier. I came over to your flat, the day you got out of hospital, to tell you and your dad I knew who did it, but I . . . I chickened out.'

I remember him walking by when I was battling in the street with the new wheelchair for the first time.

'Still,' I say, 'you didn't have to say anything. It was brave of you.'

There are a few beats of awkward silence and then

Linford speaks again, his voice quiet.

'You were right, you know. What you said that day, I mean.'

'Huh?' I've got no idea what he's talking about.

'When you said I was scared. Behind the hard front I put on at school.'

'I'm sorry . . .' I swallow, feeling bad. 'I shouldn't have said that in front of everyone.'

'But you were right.' I hear him take a big breath in. 'I went to see her, Cal, that counsellor.'

'*You* went to see Freya?' I gasp.

He laughs. 'Yeah, I know, and I was really scared of her, too – scared she'd make me talk about stuff I didn't want to think about. But she helped me find out why I was so angry all the time. She's even getting Dad some help, too.' He hesitates. 'It's still not exactly happy families in our house – he's a stubborn so-and-so. Insists he doesn't need any help. But Freya doesn't give up on people, does she?'

'No, she doesn't,' I say, but I'm not sure he hears me.

'But he's stopped drinking and he starts a new labouring job on a local building site next week.'

'Mate, I hope everything works out for you,' I say. 'I really mean that.'

And I'm surprised to find I do. I really do mean it.

'Yeah. Cheers.'

I hear Dad shout me again.

'Listen, I've got to go, but maybe we can hang out some time, yeah?'

'Maybe. Me and Dad have got to go to a meeting with Mr Fox and the governors. Freya's coming with us. I don't think they'll let me back in school because of the trouble with the police and stuff . . .' Linford's voice sounds a bit hollow and lost. 'Anyway, look after yourself, mate.'

And he ends the call.

I sit on the bed and stare at the wall for a few moments.

A lot of stuff has changed for me in the short time since I stopped hanging out with Linford. It doesn't take long to start looking at things in a different way if you start listening to your own thoughts instead of what other people are telling you to think.

I don't reckon me and Linford will ever be close again, but that's OK. We don't need to be best mates to get along.

I swing my legs over the side of the bed and reach for my crutches. It's been a month now, since the accident. I'm far from being back to normal, but I'm getting there. Slowly.

I hobble down the hallway and stop at the living-room door.

Dad's holding up a white envelope with neat, printed handwriting.

'It's addressed to you,' he says. 'Open it.'

I never get any letters.

I look at it.

Angie and Sergei sit side by side, grinning at me. I shoot Sergei a look that says, *What is it?* But he just shrugs.

I sit down and Dad hands me the letter.

I open the A4 sheet folded neatly inside and read the first few lines silently.

'Come on, then,' Dad says with a grin. 'Don't keep us in suspense.'

'It won.' I gasp. 'My screenplay, it's won the Expressions competition.'

And then there's all this whooping and hugging and Dad takes the letter and reads it out loud in a booming, theatrical voice.

'It's going to be performed,' he announces. 'A proper production with actors, like.'

'I did it,' I whisper. 'I really did it.'

Sergei grins and high-fives me.

'Remember, Calum? People *like us* can do things *like that*, when we believe we can.'

'A PLACE I WANT TO GO'
by CALUM BROOKS

1. EXT. ST ANN'S HOUSING ESTATE – DAY
BOY walks down the street of the estate
where he has lived all his life. He
sees the same people every day. Nothing
changes.

He sits on the kerbside and watches people
going about their business. He feels inside
his jacket pocket and pulls out a notebook
and pen.

People begin coming out of their houses
and walking towards him. Other kids from
school, Mrs Brewster, the hippies from
down the road. A posh lad and his thugs.
They all crowd around him and speak in
unison.

ESTATE CROWD
You were born here. You live here. You're
just a lad with silly dreams. You're not
going anywhere.

BOY stands up and opens his notebook. He

begins to read from it, shouting at the top
of his voice.

                    BOY
    'I'm me and nobody else; and whatever
      people think I am or say I am, that's
    what I'm not, because they don't know a
    thing about me.' That's an Alan Sillitoe
    quote. He was a Nottingham writer. *He* went
                    somewhere.

CUT TO:
2. EXT. LONDON – DAY
The Shard. March, weak sunshine.

Noise from city below. White, fluffy clouds
and sharp blue sky above.

BOY and his BEST FRIEND stand on the open-
air Skydeck on Floor 72. Boy looks up
with wonder at the sky through the sharp,
mirrored top slice of The Shard and then
down at the blue-grey Thames, weaving
its way through the buildings and across
London.

BOY

It feels like we could stretch up and touch
the clouds.

BEST FRIEND

It does. Let's try.

The boys stretch up as far as they can.
Wriggling their fingers towards the sky.

BOY

I can't believe I'm here. I never
thought I'd actually stand this high up.
It feels like a million miles from
home. It feels like the top of
the world.

BEST FRIEND

And now you are here, and you can see it is
real.

BOY

I suppose everything starts with an idea.

He holds up his notebook and pen.

                            BOY
        I can go anywhere I want to with these.
        I can tell people's stories. Write about
                real people from real places.

                        BEST FRIEND
                And it all starts from home.

END SCENE.

Acknowledgements

As always, I have been really fortunate to have so many supportive and talented people around me!

I'd like to give a special thank you to Lucy Pearse at Macmillan, who has worked tirelessly with me on editing the book and has given such useful suggestions and advice. Also thanks to Rachel Kellehar, who contributed to early ideas and edit notes before heading off on her maternity leave. Now the book has arrived, and so has her gorgeous new baby son, Rory!

Huge thanks to the whole team at Macmillan Children's Books, especially to Rachel Vale and the MCB design department, and to illustrator Helen Crawford-White for the wonderful covers that showcase my stories so beautifully. Special thanks to Marta Dziurosz, who kindly acted as my beta reader for this title and gave very useful guidance, and to Nick de Somogyi for his most excellent copy-editing skills.

Thank you to my agent, Clare Wallace, for her ongoing support and guidance in my writing career, and to everyone at Darley Anderson Children's Agency, especially Mary Darby and Emma Winter for their work in getting my Young Adult stories out to eight foreign territories so far.

Heartfelt thanks to the wonderful librarians and booksellers who support and recommend my books, and to my young readers who are always so full of enthusiasm and amazing questions when I visit them in schools and academies!

Huge thanks as always go to all my family, and especially to my husband Mac for his constant and unswerving support in my writing career.

This book is set in Nottinghamshire, the place I was born and have lived all my life. Local readers should be aware that I sometimes take the liberty of changing street names or geographical details to suit the story!

If you would like more information about or help with any of the issues covered in the book there are many excellent resources that can be accessed by searching online or, alternatively, ask a parent, teacher or librarian for help.

Finally, thank YOU for reading *928 Miles from Home*! Please see my website to keep up to speed with my latest writing news.

www.kimslater.com

Read on for an exclusive extract from *The Boy Who Lied*

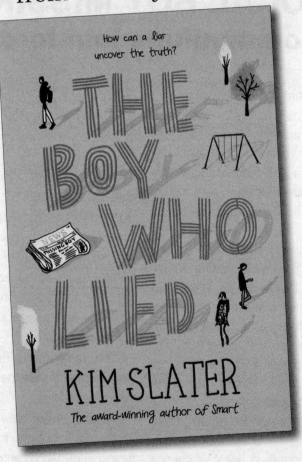

How can a liar uncover the truth?

THE BOY WHO LIED

NEWS MISSING BOY

KIM SLATER

The award-winning author of *Smart*

NOTTINGHAM POST

LOCAL BOY MISSING
Communities join forces

Yesterday, police praised Bulwell residents and the surrounding communities for their help in searching for missing 8-year-old local boy Samuel Clayton.

The boy, known to friends and family as Sam, went missing late on Sunday afternoon while visiting Bulwell Hall Park with his 14-year-old brother, Edward.

Due to an accident involving Sam's brother falling from play equipment, police say it is still not clear exactly how Sam went missing.

Within hours of his disappearance, community leaders organized a local gathering through social media, where over 200 volunteers took part in a three-hour fingertip search of the park and nearby woodland.

Police would like to question a bearded man of dishevelled appearance with light-brown short hair who was seen in the area shortly before Sam's disappearance. He wore a checked shirt and beige trousers tucked into tan-coloured boots.

Door-to-door enquiries and a wider search are expected to take place today.

Anyone who saw Sam at the park or who has any further information can contact Nottinghamshire Police.

It's the day after my brother went missing, and I am alone in a small white room.

My heartbeat is thumping in my throat and I feel sick and tired.

I can't hear the usual hospital-type noises or the hushed pad of soft shoes as the nurses dash about. Instead, there's a hum of frantic voices growing steadily louder outside the closed door. Someone shouts and then there's a scuffling noise.

A thump on the door makes my heartbeat blip. It sounds like someone just fell against it. I don't move.

I'm facing away from the door and lying on my right-hand side because it hurts to keep turning my neck. I think I must have twisted it when I fell. From here, I can stare out of the small window to the bushes beyond.

I've seen those kinds of bushes before; there are purple flowers on them that attract butterflies. We learned about plants in Biology during the spring term, but I can't remember the name of this one. Instead, I focus on trying to remember all the chemical symbols and the important dates in our history project, but all the facts feel chewed up together in my mind.

Still, it's better than thinking about why I'm here in the hospital. About what happened yesterday afternoon . . . Anything is better than that.

The noise outside dies down and then the door opens. I squeeze my eyes shut and pretend to be asleep.

'Ahh, admiring our lovely buddleia, I see.' I hear Dr Wood walk around to the bottom of the bed. 'You've got the best room here, you know. Best view, anyhow.'

I open my eyes again. Outside, the butterflies flit around, showing off like they know we're admiring them. I spot a couple of red speckled woods and a brimstone. And I'm sure there was a red admiral out there, just before I closed my eyes.

What does it matter?

'I'm sorry about the disturbance,' Dr Wood says briskly. 'Somehow the press got on to the ward. Very resourceful, they are. Turn up at visiting time, you see, and slip in with the genuine families.'

'Is Mum OK?' I ask.

When the two reporters and a cameraman had appeared at the door fifteen minutes ago, Mum had dashed out of the room, pale and panicky.

'We're from the *Nottingham Post*,' one of them blurted out urgently. 'Can you tell us what happened at the park yesterday, Ed? Do you often take your brother out alone?'

'Get out!' Mum had screeched. 'Isn't there any security in this place?'

Charlie pushed the photographer, who had said the F-word about ten times when his lens had slipped out of his hand and smashed on the floor.

Nurses and doctors had come running, and the quiet space had suddenly seemed very crowded and noisy. Through it all, the woman kept shouting questions at me. Then two policemen appeared and escorted the reporters out.

I pulled the sheet up over my head and waited until the sickly feeling passed.

Dr Wood stops moving and looks at me. 'Your mum is fine, Ed. The family liaison worker is with her right now, but she'll be back soon. Did you want me to call your neighbour Charlie in?'

'No,' I say quickly.

Dr Wood turns and plucks the clipboard from the bottom of my bed.

'I don't remember what happened at the park,' I say for about the hundredth time, my eyes prickling. I'm saying it as much to myself as to him. 'Honest, I don't.'

'You probably will regain your memory.' The doctor looks up from studying the paperwork. 'Sadly, it can't be rushed. It'll come back when it's good and ready and—'

'But what about our Sam? What if he's –' My voice cracks as I interrupt him and a tear traces down my cheek. I hope it gets absorbed into the pillow before Dr Wood notices.

'I know the police are going to be talking to you, trying to help you to remember, and that's important. Then you'll be in the best possible position to help your brother.'

I sniff.

'Good news. Your readings are nice and stable now.' He scribbles something on a sheet of paper and hooks the clipboard back on the bed rail. 'In fact, we can probably get you home later today.'

'Home?' I try to swallow down the lump that's just appeared in my throat, but it doesn't budge.

'There's no sense in you lying here bored out of your mind now we've checked you out. And I bet you'd much rather be comfy back at home on your Xbox, eh?'

He grins and winks, and somehow I manage a weak smile.

I think about our cold house, with its peeling wallpaper and draughty windows.

I think about how we've never had an Xbox.

I think about how we hardly ever even get to watch a full programme on the TV because the electric usually runs out before the end.

About the author

Kim Slater honed her storytelling skills as a child, writing macabre tales specially designed to scare her younger brother! Taking her literary inspiration from everyday life, Kim's debut novel, *Smart*, won more than ten regional prizes and has been shortlisted for over twenty regional and national awards, including the Waterstones Children's Book Prize and the Federation of Children's Book Groups Prize. *Smart* was also longlisted for the 2015 CILIP Carnegie Medal. She has written four novels for Macmillan Children's Books set in her home town of Nottingham, where she lives with her husband.

www.kimslater.com

Also by Kim Slater

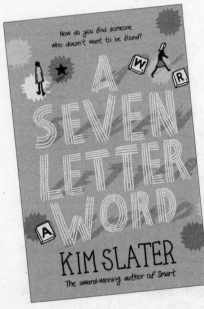